# Born Freeloaders

## Also by Phumlani Pikoli

*The Fatuous State of Severity* (2018, 2016)

'Hauntingly engaging.'
– Thandiwe Ntshingila, *The South African*

'Crisp, experimental and beautifully weird.'
– Phumlani S. Langa, *City Press*

'Phumlani Pikoli's collection of short stories deals with the contemporary South African reality in a way that is absurdist and, bizarrely, beautifully familiar.'
– Kwanele Sosibo, *Mail & Guardian*

# Born Freeloaders

A NOVEL

## Phumlani Pikoli

PICADOR AFRICA

First published in 2019
by Picador Africa
an imprint of Pan Macmillan South Africa
Private Bag X19, Northlands
Johannesburg
2116

www.panmacmillan.co.za

ISBN 9781770106796
e-ISBN 9781770106802

© Phumlani Pikoli 2019

All rights reserved. No part of this publication may be reproduced, stored in or introduced into a retrieval system, or transmitted, in any form, or by any means (electronic, mechanical, photocopying, recording or otherwise), without the prior written permission of the publisher. Any person who does any unauthorised act in relation to this publication may be liable to criminal prosecution and civil claims for damages.

*This is a work of fiction. Any resemblance to places or events or actual persons, living or dead, is purely coincidental.*

Editing by Katlego Tapala
Proofreading by Sean Fraser
'Children without Tongues' illustration by Lisolomzi Pikoli
Design and typesetting by Triple M Design, Johannesburg
Cover design by K4

Printed by **novus print**, a division of Novus Holdings

For
*Silumko*
*Wandile*
*Mad Voodoo*
*Phat Few*
*and*
*the rest of Andile's Bored Company (ABC)*

'You know the whole 1994 negotiation?'
I looked at him.
'What do you think Mandela and those guys actually bought in that whole thing? Cause the gains are way too small for that to have just been it.'
I sipped my beer and shrugged.
'They bought us ... We are the settlement.'

Uncle Zweli was Xolani's father's brother. He moved into the house when Nthabiseng was four and Xolani eight. He lived with their mother and Nthabiseng's father, Graham, for some time. On Uncle Zweli's arrival, Xolani believed he was seeing a ghost that had come to grant him his wishes. It was on an afternoon when he and his little sister had found some wood that the builders at the house had left out over the weekend. They had always wanted a treehouse, and their parents kept promising to build them one but never did. Ausi Linda had chased them outside to go play, while she cleaned the house. Their parents had left early and when the children realised that the building materials had been left lonely, they thought to keep them company. While inspecting the wood and rumbling through some tools that they could use, they heard the gate opening, the car slowly driving down the winding driveway and parking in the carport next to the one that they had been preparing to build their house in. Their parents were first to exit, with smiles and hints at a surprise visitor. He stepped out of the car with small curls gelled to his head. On the sides of his face, his beard resembled lamb chops, with a smile that spread from one to the other. He shifted his weight onto one leg, took a drag of the cigarette held between his thumb, middle and index fingers, and looked at the pair whose work his arrival had interrupted. Nthabiseng was puzzled by his sudden appearance. Xolani wasted no time, ran to him and leapt into his arms. Zweli caught the child who had screamed 'Daddy' at him in mid-air and held the excited little boy who had never met his father, swinging him around. His little sister found her brother's enthusiasm infectious and she too wanted to enjoy the moment Xoli was having with the stranger. She too was lifted into the stranger's arms and received kisses from him.

'This is my daddy!' Xolani told his little sister excitedly! 'He's finally home!' No one had the heart to break the joy of the moment and so they let him believe it.

When the illusion was shattered later that day, Xolani refused to believe the truth that was being forced on him. He never got completely used to the fact that the new presence in the house, who so closely resembled the face in the photo albums, was in fact his father's younger brother and not his father. As time wore on, he played along with what everyone told him, but was convinced in secret that Uncle Zweli was his father.

Uncle Zweli always had a smile fixed on his face. He didn't sleep very much, the pair noticed; always up at odd hours of the night fixing himself cups of tea and heading outside to smoke his special cigarettes, that smelled sour to their noses. Inside, he smoked normal cigarettes. Over time they began to register a certain stiffness from their parents when they spoke about Uncle Zweli's special cigarettes and his ways after smoking one. He'd often ramble incoherently at the dinner table, or giggle to himself unexpectedly. Masechaba would often bring him back to the present moment with gentle interruptions. Before, everyone including Ausi Linda had laughed and joked about it. But increasingly the only adult who had continued to smile about the cigarettes was Uncle Zweli himself.

'My children without tongues,' Uncle Zweli would call the sibling pair.

'We have tongues!' Nthabiseng shouted at Uncle Zweli. He drained himself of a slow laughter at her petulance, took the children into the garden where he rolled himself a cigarette and told them a story as they all sat on the grass.

## EDUCATION

*The Children without Tongues lived throughout the ages of humanity, stretching all the way back to the first people to leave the seas. In fact, they watched Fish emerge from water and turn into tree-climbing monkeys. They had helped with this transformation, in exchange for a promise that they in turn would be taught how to breathe underwater. The Children trusted in the balance that governed the worlds of water and land. Without land, water could not exist as it served no purpose. And*

*water could not exist where it was not needed. Water existed to give birth to land, as without water, land could not live. The sky had always made clear its capricious nature and The Children accepted its vacillations and their own restriction to the mountain tops.*

*When The Fish first surfaced with caution, seeking out the invisible presence of the air, it was to the great distaste of the ocean currents that sought to eternally cover The Fish and shield them from the air that sought to dry their scales. There were some Fish that submitted to the possessive nature of the currents. However, many of them continued in their efforts and it was into these turbulent waters that the fighting Fish released their eggs. The tiny Aquarians emerged from their bubbles with muscles that the school preceding them had been unable to develop.*

*As the passage of time eroded the rocks of the mountain, The Children found that the ground they inhabited had come closer to the ocean. The shortened distance gave them sight of the growing presence of silver beyond the edges of their shores. Mystery within arm's reach had always been cause for investigation, with cessation from material animation an accepted part of each Child's departure from home. Return belonged to those who left, and those who never left were never missed.*

*Some of The Children who had left returned home with tales of the new creatures being forged in the waters. Without hesitation, scores of Children lined the shores to investigate the waters from which they never drank. By the time they reached the shoreline – after a night's walk – the morning sun slowly slithered over the bodies of the strange silver-scaled souls washed ashore. The silver beings wriggled and sputtered. Their bodies thrashed on the wet sand with a savagery that defied the morning's serenity. It was understood by The Children that these strangers to land needed to be thrown back into the froth from which they dribbled. A purely pity-laden instinct. The Fish that returned to the sea excreted eggs that hatched ashore.*

*The creatures that emerged out of these eggs shrieked with a sonic nightmare born of lung and gill. The Children accepted that the years they had spent throwing The Fish back had made the strangers persevere and understood that The Fish desired to share the land. The Children, therefore, anticipated that their own voyages beneath the surface of the water would be met with the same benevolence.*

*The ear-piercing racket lulled into the temporal landscape, along with the land-incongruent features of The Fish. The Fish grew arms, then legs, before climbing trees. The phrase 'Like a fish in the tree' became a common reference for perseverance.*

\*

She stepped out of the shower and reached for a towel on the rack just outside the glass door. Vigorously rubbing her locks, she gazed into the mirror and sneered at her reflection, widening her glassy red eyes as much as she could. The colour was a reminder of the previous night's debauchery, as was the mild headache and the sour taste of dehydration. She was used to going out on school nights (as long as her parents were out of town, which was often enough). Happy with the shampoo that had removed the smell of smoke out of her hair, she dried off the rest of her body. Songs from the previous night burrowed their way into her ear and she hummed the tunes all through the dry-off, the popping in of her contact lenses and teeth-brushing process. A memory of Priscilla's arms around her brother's neck flashed in front of her eyes and she found herself getting annoyed. The last thing she wanted was the broken school bicycle trying to get her brother to take a ride. She suppressed the feeling by distracting herself and turned her head to look out the window. She was greeted by the warmth of sunlight that aligned itself with the bathroom's tile markings. Her clean teeth let her smile send a reflection greeting the sun back. As if awaiting that signal, the star asserted its light and filled the entire bathroom. Usually, after such a heavy night, this would have been too bright for her, but not today.

'Thank you for sending my parents away,' she jokingly told the star.

She let herself out the bathroom and enjoyed the Medusa-like shadow she cast on the opposing wall. It had become one of the things she looked forward to most about opening her bathroom door in the summer shower steam. She turned towards the end of the hall, making her way to her room and took a second to take in the family portrait that hung at the end of the hallway. It always struck her that she was the only one who was smiling in the photo.

Her father wore his hair in a buzz cut. This, together with his stark blue eyes, was often intimidating to those who did not know him. He had earned the nickname Rosy, which often irritated him but had stuck. He was a man of minimal smiles and words. But it was often when he had had a few drinks that his cheeks and ears gained a pinkish tinge, hence the handle. Nthabiseng would tease her dad with this nickname when she felt cheeky.

Next, she took in her mother, Masechaba, who scrutinised the camera dead on, with her husband beside her. Her dreadlocks were tied in a ponytail and her eyes held a confident stare, her mouth almost smiling. Nthabiseng had always loved and envied her mother's dark skin and saw it as the definition of strength. Her mother's hand was resting on her brother's shoulder. Xolani sat in front of his mother and next to Nthabiseng, whose elbow rested on his knee. Her brother's skin matched her mother's. He wore no smile in the photo. Rather, he stared blankly into the camera. Nthabiseng leaned on her older brother's knee and exposed a smile with a few missing teeth. She thought back on the smiling child whose memory had started taking notes that she'd later recall at random times. There'd be things passed that made her feel odd but that she could not explain. Casual comments on the way she looked and conducted herself that made her feel as if she was more noticeable than other children. In later years, she felt that these were indicators of how special she was. However, later on she realised that the remarks had, in fact, isolated her from her peers. As the years wore on, the notes changed from other learners needing to be more like her to her needing to take the responsibility of knowing better.

She had also found herself to be popular amongst her peers. While she was a coveted prize in school, this came with its own anxieties that were never expressed to anyone but her brother. She felt the need to always be the first to know of something and have it. Others seemed to come to her for advice. When she didn't like someone, others would turn their backs on them too. It was a burdensome power she had neither sought out nor relinquished. She merely accepted the divine right to rule without questioning the authority it afforded her. She took for granted the way that she could affect her peers and ruled rather carelessly. Feeling removed from most of the other children, she didn't easily empathise with their problems and listened to them with more curiosity than emotion. She wasn't particularly difficult or hard to get along with. It was more about things that she disliked on a whim without much explanation. It was the other children around her that had given her the enigmatic, knowledgeable, charming and aloof persona she carried from the beginning of primary school.

'What are you?' – more of an accusation than a question – defined her; the instant reduction in many an introduction. A curiosity that lumbered with many an eye encountered. She was nothing if not assigned a label by anyone other than herself. She was fixed to the ideas of others that shaped her and thus illusive to being assigned permanence.

'Nthabiseng?' Her name repeated on first impressions.

'Are you sure?' would be the next attempt to change her person. Before calling her by her name, some teachers had referred to her as 'Monique se kleurling maatjie'.

She assumed that the unanimous recognition from her educators had been passed on by her brother's veteran status as a troublesome Grade 5 pupil. In one of her reports to her parents at the dinner table she had casually dropped the nickname given to her by her educators.

'Hmm …' her mother had said, carefully eating her food without releasing the smile on her face.

'What's your teacher's name again?' her father suddenly asked her.

The conversation was diverted to other school activities and dinner passed with barely a word uttered from her brother, in keeping with his character.

She hardly noticed the teachers' change in demeanour. They were suddenly short with her and tried to be more stringent with the rules than they were with other children. This was overall an exercise without results as she was a diligent pupil with a popularity that rarely came into check. And so her brother found himself on the receiving end of the teachers' increased surly attitudes since the arrival of his little sister.

*

In her bedroom she pressed Play on her i-dock and tossed her towel aside. The swing jazz led her hips to sway from one side to the other and her legs to move to the rhythm, singing along as she got dressed. She looked in the mirror and saw a dreadlocked, green-socked, black-shoed, green-tied, white-shirted girl staring back at her. She placed her index and middle fingers together and pressed them against her lips and then flicked her wrist to one side. She watched one leg lift in the reflection as she picked up her bag and blazer, leaving the room.

'Ag, maar jy lees mooi. Dankie Nthabiseng, jy kan maar sit. Pragtig my skat, dit was wonderlik. Leonard, môre begin ons met jou. Goed, staan op. Totsiens almal. Julle mag loop. Kut-legoo kan ek asseblief met jou praat?'

'Jeez Nthabiseng, what you do to get that right?' Monique asked, opening a packet of sour jellybeans, as they walked out of class.

'I don't know. She's probably trying to get her kids free tickets to one of my brother's shows.' Walking towards the bridge that joined the school's C and D blocks they caught sight of the others. Monique's retort was drowned out by the guys' raucous shouting about Saturday's rugby game. Joan emerged from the huddle of large teenage males, bug eyed and gasping for air. She lunged a hug at both Nthabiseng and Monique to express her relief.

'I'm so glad to see you guys! You won't believe how long I had to listen to this! First, Tumi didn't come to school, then Mr Prince was absent and so I had to listen to this all through invigilation! I mean, ja, I get why they like it, but to have an hour-long screaming match just to carry it with you into break is ridiculous!'

'Jesus, are you breathing yet?' Monique said,

dropping her jaw and exposing the mash of jellybeans for effect.

'Ag, that's disgusting! Anyway, how was Afrikaans with Ms Van de Watt? Has she finally changed her tampon brand?'

'I think she actually might have,' Nthabiseng replied pleasantly.

'At least for her,' said Monique, 'she's convinced that Van de Watt's trying to suck up to her in the hopes of getting into Xolani's good books.'

'Jealousy is unbecoming, Monique,' Joan sang. Monique had another response, stifled by the guys bursting into a new round of shouting.

'Fuck that shit! Junior Roux had his time, bring in the new blood: Thabang Bengu is the heat!' Siya shouted. 'Thabang Bengu is the only number one in the world who also serves as a loose forward. He's like having two players in one. So whatever team he plays for has sixteen men on the field.'

'Ag, that just means he wastes energy running around the field and ends up too tired to push in the scrum,' Pieter condescended.

'Who cares? Rugby is just a game that gives men an excuse to touch each other!' Monique yelled while pushing herself through the huddle. This brought on a cacophonous frenzy about the manliness of the sport. Monique had a habit of pouring gas on a flame and she loved it. The guys loved it too. She smirked as she began her descent of the staircase, crumpling her empty sweet packet. A group of Grade 8 girls charged up the staircase, pressing Monique up against the wall as they squealed and giggled. They immediately stopped at the sight of Nthabiseng. She crossed her arms and let her bag drop and hang off her forearm.

'What's going on?' she asked shortly. A little girl with a row of badges on each fold of the front of her green blazer sheepishly stepped forward. Her thin little legs edged onward one centimetre at a time towards Nthabiseng, while the others moved backwards down the staircase at the same pace. Her eyes tried to evade Nthabiseng's glare.

'Sorry Mam, Richard was chasing us. He has a mouse that he's trying to put down our shirts,' she stuttered.

'Can you see the matric in the stairwell that you've almost completely squashed into the wall?' Nthabiseng asked. The group of girls collectively gasped and made rushed apologies. Monique waved them off.

'Jeandre. You're an RCL member.'

'Yes Mam, I am,' the girl replied.

'And what does RCL stand for?' Nthabiseng pressed.

'It stands for the Representative Council for Learners, Mam,' she replied, her voice getting quieter with each word she spoke.

'You're playing on the staircase during break when you know that it's out of bounds.'

'Yes Mam,' Jeandre replied with a whisper and a sniff.

'Next time, it's pink slips for all of you. Now, off you go.'

A chorus of 'Yes Mams' and 'Sorry Mams' was made, and the girls rushed back down the staircase. Jeandre shuffled along behind them. The sound of the girls erupting into excited laughter once they got to the bottom could be heard.

'Gotta say, I love watching you in full prefect action mode. Especially with a hangover,' Siya chirped.

'Yeah … I know,' Nthabiseng responded nonchalantly. She slowly started making her way down the staircase.

'Let's go get lunch and sit out on the field,' Monique gave her a faint smile as a means of saying thank you.

'It's okay,' Nthabiseng whispered as she walked past.

'Last night was amazing! They were too nice,' the sound of a random voice landed in her ear.

They were all talking about it. She knew they would be. She got tired of it. Between her friends getting the lyrics and songs wrong, the guys competing to prove who took the most shots and the baking sun, something had to give.

'I'm going to the tuck-shop.' She got up and grabbed her bottled water as she embarked on a noisy climb down the metal supporters' stands they were sitting on. Each thud produced a loud clang under her rubber-soled shoes, the echoes filling the ears of all those sitting close by. She momentarily attracted the attention of everyone sitting on the field. She was used to being watched. She was familiar with the feeling of having everyone's eyes on her. The focus no longer fazed her. She knew that the guys were also watching. They were attracted to her; she knew that. No matter how platonic the relationship seemed to be, the attraction was there.

Joan asked her to buy her a bottle of water. Nthabiseng raised a finger above her head without turning back, acknowledging the request. Walking on the athletic track, she felt the sun licking the back of her neck. She put a hand to it to soothe it somewhat. She felt her phone vibrate. *Just on time*, she thought to herself. She pulled it out and answered.

'Right on cue. Tuck-shop,' she said, and dropped the call.

She walked past the school pool and saw a group of boys huddled in a corner, probably playing dice.

'What's the school coming to?' she said aloud. She sped up as she tried to pass a group of girls sitting by the rock just outside the school's drama department. She stopped and slowly turned around as she heard one of them calling her by a pet name. She anticipated the conversation that would follow and cursed herself for forgetting her earphones. A sweet, fake smile crept onto her face. A tall and skinny blonde girl wearing lip gloss and visible mascara showed off her brilliant white teeth. The sweet and high-pitched tone hit Nthabiseng's ears.

'Nthabi, babes, how are you?'

'I'm fine Priscilla, how are you?'

Her perfume filled Nthabiseng's nostrils as Priscilla wrapped her long, skinny arms around Nthabiseng's short and small frame. Priscilla pressed her lips on both of her cheeks.

The image of Priscilla's arms around her brother's neck returned. She was once again irritated that Priscilla still felt it appropriate to attend his events even after Nthabiseng had allowed a huge distance to grow between them.

To cut the physical exchange short, Nthabiseng resorted to asking her again how she was doing.

'I'm fine, I'm fine! What are you doing? Why are you walking by yourself? Why don't you come sit with us? Your brother's show last night was so awesome! Please come sit with us Nthabi …'

She looked at the other six girls she'd intensely disliked throughout her school career. They in turn disliked her. She saw them as the lip-sticked, high-heeled, short-skirted (school or not) prima donna kind, who only went for guys already in tertiary, and had done so since they were fourteen. They, in turn, saw her as an uptight jock girl with a silver spoon in her mouth.

*

Nthabiseng and Priscilla had struck up an unexpected friendship a few years earlier on a school camping trip. As with most people in her grade, they had gone to the same primary school but had never really interacted with each other. The two had lived dissimilar parallel lives, which had resulted in an unspoken and effective apathy for one another. While they never had reason for bad blood, because they were not friends and did not know each other for much of their school career, they both assumed that they were not fond of each other.

Priscilla's profile was plagued by rumours of a dysfunctional home, drug use and an early sex life. Her school attendance was sporadic at best, yet she scraped through each grade with the exact marks needed to pass. Loved to be hated by both students and teachers alike, most of her peers feared her because of the life they believed she led, which did not match their own experiences in gated community homes. The people she hung out with had the same kind of reputations; Priscilla and her ilk always referred to themselves as outcasts and seemed intent on reinforcing their status to anyone who cared to question it. By the time Nthabiseng and Priscilla were forced into the same group on their Grade 10 school camping trip they hadn't anticipated the possibility of forming a sincere friendship – even though that would later fizzle out.

'It was my brother's friend who did it. I mean, I

was, like, twelve, so it's not really that bad. Cause I felt something for him. I just wasn't completely sure about it, but I still think that I actually wanted it and I definitely thought he was fucking hot,' Priscilla began.

Nthabiseng squinted at her in the dark as she passed her the joint. The moon and starlit sky were their main sources of light behind the dormitory. Priscilla poked her head around the corner, making sure they were still safe. The sound of crickets punctuated their inhalations. Looking at Priscilla, Nthabiseng made out her silhouette and her long, thin strands of hair dyed silver by the celestial lights. She and her friends had always referred to Priscilla as 'the bag of bones'. On that night, she was listening to the bones chatter with a precarious nonchalance, confusing Nthabiseng's clouded mind with regard to appropriately timed responses.

'The first time he put it in my arse I fucking screamed! Jesus Christ! He didn't even warn me.' She took the joint from Nthabiseng's hand and dragged. The ember at the end lit up the tip of her nose. She inhaled and giggled, 'Yoh, it took me, like, a whole day to be able to sit on my arse again.'

'You were twelve and he was sixteen?' Nthabiseng asked.

'Yeah ...' Priscilla said, her teeth reflecting the moon in the same silver her hair shone in. 'What, your brother and his friends never believed in the "Anything after twelve is lunch" rule?' Priscilla gave a nervous giggle as Nthabiseng let the realisation crawl down her throat and tried to steady the discomfort rising in her stomach. She drew a deep breath and forced a whispered laugh.

'But what about your parents?' she asked, trying to mask her concern and feign calm.

'Ja, that was fucked up. My dad beat the shit out of my brother with his gun when he found out. He kicked my brother out of the house that day.'

'That's so hectic,' she quietly muttered, more to herself than to Priscilla.

'I mean, Dad is a fucking arsehole anyway, so I was fucking pissed off. Cause I really, really liked the guy and I knew what I was doing. What pisses me off is that the jerk doesn't even know me. It's not like he even cares, it was just a way for him to feel good about himself about keeping me for himself or whatever. He never wanted me to do anything by myself. He hasn't even let me see my mom for, like, almost three years.'

'How did he find out?' Nthabiseng pressed with nervous apprehension, fearfully mesmerised by the details of Priscilla's life. She'd heard about Priscilla's mother's alcoholism and how she lived in a dump where all sorts of people came and went. She'd even heard a rumour, that she was sure wasn't true, that her brother and mother had had some sort of incestuous relationship. While she and Monique spent their holidays going to Ratanga Junction and on trips to Zanzibar with Monique's father, Priscilla was being turned into an adult.

'Oh shit, here comes Ms Snyman,' Priscilla whispered hastily.

The pair had been hiding behind the dormitory they shared as a result of being assigned to the same group. The trip was apparently about breaking down the cliquey nature of the grade, to get them out of their comfort zones and mingle with others outside of their long-established little clusters. They were even forced to eat meals in their camp groups.

Luckily, the joint had already been completely smoked, so they just needed to throw away the roach. As the beam of the torch made its way past the wall they stood behind, they carefully tried to sneak their shoes on the pebbled sand without making a noise. With their heightened senses, everything underfoot sounded like a crash. They could hear the footsteps of their stern-faced, auburn-haired tormentor shuffling to delight in clamping down on their delinquency. They rounded their corner as she rounded hers. They found themselves under the spotlight of the front veranda of their dorm room, which faced the open lawn framed by the other girls' dorm rooms. They hesitated next to the dorm's front door. The creaking sound of the handle opening the metal door would be an obvious giveaway that would surely alert the teacher to their presence.

Nthabiseng was breathing rapidly and feared the impending consequences of being discovered by her biology teacher. The paranoia carried her imagination to the moment of her parents being called and informed of her drug-taking on a school outing. Looking up at Priscilla didn't comfort Nthabiseng, because her company would have been the proof of her dabble with delinquency. Priscilla looked down at her and smiled as they pressed their backs against the cold face-brick wall they needed to urgently be behind. They could hear their teacher's steps making their way around the back of the dorm, tracing their path.

'Get inside, get into your bed and leave the door open,' Priscilla whispered to Nthabiseng.

'What?' she said back to her, listening to each step of the rapidly approaching teacher.

'Now!' Priscilla said in a loud-enough whisper that forced Nthabiseng to act without thinking. She immediately turned, open the door, took four giant steps and crawled under the covers without taking off her shoes. Outside, she heard Ms Snyman confront Priscilla. Breathing heavily, she heard the two other members in the dorm move around because of the disturbance.

'What's going on?' Louise asked.

Nthabiseng tried to keep her breathing down, while listening to what was being said outside. The other two picked up on the tension and didn't press.

'Are you saying that I can't go to the bathroom?!'

Priscilla shouted from the doorway.

'Ag, just stop your nonsense, Priscilla! It's after bedtime and you're not supposed to be outside! I can smell the cigarette on you!'

'What are you talking about? What cigarettes? This is the sweater I was wearing by the campfire and I just went to go pee!'

Nthabiseng tried several times to breathe through her nose and swallow her heart down back into place. She imagined Ms Snyman realising that what she was, in fact, smelling, was not cigarettes at all. She wished Priscilla would stop arguing with her and just get into the dorm.

'Jy dink jy's slim! Empty your pockets.'

Priscilla turned her pockets inside out and nothing fell out of them. Nthabiseng realised that she had Priscilla's lighter in her pocket and immediately panicked at the thought of the teacher storming in and searching the dormitory to make her point.

'You see? Now, can I just go to the frikkin bathroom already?' Priscilla said with a smug irritation in her voice.

'Watch how you speak to me! Go! Hurry up!' Ms Snyman shouted at her before banging the metal door shut.

The relief Nthabiseng felt was not instant. She still had lingering thoughts of being caught. She swore to herself in her panic that she wouldn't smoke weed again under such risky circumstances. She listened to the others snigger and mutter about the close call. She tried uncomfortably to laugh about it with them. All four were talking about how cool Priscilla was under pressure, making fun of their teacher's accent and the fact that she didn't even know what weed smelt like.

Priscilla and Nthabiseng smoked more joints on the trip without getting busted, although each night the fear and paranoia gripped Nthabiseng and she swore to herself it was the last.

*

'Um ... maybe later Prisci. I have to meet Thami at the tuck-shop,' said Nthabiseng.

'Oh ... okay then,' Priscilla replied, slightly injured.

'Well ... later then, babe.'

Priscilla repeated the motion of kissing Nthabiseng's cheeks.

As Nthabiseng spanned the quad area while moving towards the tuck-shop she spotted him. Hands in blazer pockets, the stick of a sucker standing out of his mouth, he was staring again.

'Can you stop it?' she asked him in a slightly amused voice.

To which he replied, 'Sorry, I can't help it.'

'Wouldn't you find someone constantly staring at you creepy? You still have that photo, stare at that all you like!'

'I'm in love!'

'You're obsessed! And the only reason we're still cool is cause ... well ... everybody likes being liked.' She smiled and turned to get into line.

'Yeah, but everybody already likes you. You even have a friend in the "queen of the antisocial".' He nodded in Priscilla's direction.

Nthabiseng ignored the intended provocation, 'Believe it or not Thami, there's something about you that both weirds me out and endears you to me.'

'I know, I've heard that line about a hundred times now. Pass the money, I'll get whatever you want. You don't have to stand in this mess.'

She looked at the bunched-up students shoving to get to the front of the line, shouting their orders at the tuck-shop volunteers.

'Thank you.' She flicked two coins, one after the other, and he caught each with the same hand. As she stepped out of the line, Mr Wilcox, their principal, made his way up the corridor.

'Ahh, and here's Rochelle High's new celebrity.'

'My brother's the celebrity, sir,' she corrected him politely.

'And you're riding the coattails like a little sister would,' the blasé headmaster told her. She turned with him. He didn't spare her another glance. She took the opportunity to dig imaginary knives into his back and pictured him tripping on the step into the office, showering his papers across the floor, his face acquainting itself with the tiles.

'Forget that drunk. You keen on taking pictures today?' Thami handed her the bottle of water and dropped the change into her open palm.

'Sure, can we check out Marabastad and take pictures there? You can pick me up at three.'

'Cool, now hurry up and get back to your cool friends before one of them sees you talking to your stalker again.'

'I don't see you as much of a stalker. I prefer creep.'

'Right ... cause there's a difference. All I did was take a picture of you looking cool on the balcony from where I was standing and post it on my blog.'

'Yeah, there *is* a difference. Taking my photo without my knowledge and putting it up on your blog without my knowing is some creepy-ass shit. Now, let me get back to my cool friends before they notice I'm missing and come after you.'

As she walked away he shouted, 'I'd love nothing more than to have some enlightening conversations with those creatine-overloaded Sartre fanatics!'

She turned back to face him, tilting her head to one side with her dreadlocks hanging and almost touching her shoulder. She half closed her eyes and seemed to pout. The same look he always got when he said something that impressed her. She slowly sang to him, 'Careful what you wish for, Thami. Three o'clock. Don't be late.' Then she turned around and walked away without looking back.

*

Waking up in Bell's room disorientated him a bit. He was not yet used to the concept of having a girlfriend and still felt some excitement when he turned over to see her lying next to him. He took her in for some time as she slept, then got out of bed. He put his boxers on and walked out into the passage towards the bathroom, his bladder extremely pressed. As he reached out to open the bathroom door without thinking to knock, he heard the shower turning on. His hand shot back and he whispered, 'Shit!' to no audience.

Thinking about the awkward disaster that could have taken place, he made his way back to Bell's room and dressed himself in the previous night's skinny jeans, engrained with the stench of the club's cigarette smoke. His best course of action was to find an inconspicuous space in the garden.

Corner found, he revelled in the opportunity to drain some of the heated poison that still coursed through him. A shake and zip-up later, he fought through the tight stiches of his upper thigh's pocket for his phone and earphones. While pulling them out he checked his newsfeed and notifications to find that a new article had been written about the band he led. Nervous excitement gripped him as he saw how many people had already shared the article from the blog, 'We Are Nothing'. It was only when he read the name of the site that his stomach turned. The article's title confirmed that the worst was to come.

'Fuck!' he said to himself.

### Black Strokes in White Privilege
Written by Donald Sterling

There's a special place on the internet that reserves the right to completely cut off the dick muscles of the undeserving, especially when they just sound like a bunch of African children that the Parlotones adopted and then sold to Madonna to make sure their next single goes platinum. These gutless Rebecca Black knock-offs blowing the whole of Ladysmith Black Mambazo on a Friday need to have their cheap antics shown for what they really are, which is not musicians, by the way. They're just another version of industry darlings, made and manufactured in the ghettos of suburban Pretoria. That's right! Just because they're black guys playing instruments and making ersatz alternative music doesn't make them real.

In an interview, the band's frontman, Xolani Jobodwana, once responded to a question about why they named their band 'The Cursed Children of Ham' with the following:

> 'We're black. There's no point hiding from that. The world will constantly remind us of that, no matter what music we make. So we might as well do it first.'

Now that we know what their selling point is, shall we get stuck in to it? Let's start with the name of the song:

**Stupid Fat Loser, Shut up and Dance!**

Obviously, they're trying to get attention with an 'edgy' sounding title, but it's all just the same bullshit PC internet politics and catchphrases that the woke circle jerks are waiting to jizz for. It's clearly fucking click bait. And all of the spunk-guzzling keyboard human rights activists were just waiting to click up a fucking storm about how offensive the title was. Of course, without actually listening to the song and realising that it was made for their coteries.

The song is just another way for people to make themselves feel better for exploiting the misfortunes of others. The lyrics tell the story of some sad fucks who hate themselves, out at a party. Intending to troll some poor guy, the pathetic, scud-sucking vermin take pictures of a fat dude at the party who is only trying to bust a couple of moves and have fun. They posted a picture of the lard in motion and then another of him looking sadly at the floor.

The caption read: 'Spotted this specimen trying to dance the other week. He stopped when he saw us laughing.'

The tale then unfolds into one of those feel-good internet viral sensations, displaying the kind of pathetic desperation that proves how great people can be when they take a moment to pause from being self-absorbed dickheads posting about crème-fraiche-salmon-croissants-filled-with-basil-and-capers-washed-down-with-Sunday-brunch-mimosas. (Did that make anyone else hungry?) Some bleeding-heart woman launched a campaign to find the fatty, buy him an air ticket to LA and throw him a party with over a thousand women committed to dancing with the guy. There was no way that the virtuous assembly of twelebs was about to let this opportunity go. So, a few celebrities jumped on the bandwagon and raised money for cyber-bullying organisations in the US and UK. I don't think there have been more boys on earth wishing that they could be bullied and bury themselves beneath all those titties. That is, of course, until: drum roll please ... The Cursed Children of Ham. (Cool name by the way, no bullshit. It's the only reason I even decided to listen to your shit.)

You know what undoes the good on earth that others do? People like this, trying to eat the icing off the cake that they made. You guys make music like you're intentionally aiming to sound like The Strokes playing through a stroke. Your private-school accents, whining on and on about how shit people can be, and shouting the command, 'Shut up and dance!' like a chocolate-flavoured Blink 182 fighting to make bad covers of Bloc Party songs, are the reason children die of cancer. The only part of the song that is vaguely cool is when you guys sing in your own language and voices. Which, unfortunately, is still not even original. My colleagues told me that even that's some nursery-school song used to make fun of fat kids on the playground. The equivalent of singing 'fatty boom boom' repeatedly. A few catchy guitar chords, some false second-line drumming and the lyrics telling a fat loser to shut up and dance and lose himself in music – cause fuck anyone laughing at you – is all it took for the kids to lose their shit. Here's the best part, all they did for their music video was to get people to post videos of themselves online trying to do the most embarrassing dance moves they could think of to the song – and bam! Another viral hit! Not only is the song milking, but they were able to rack up over a million views in the first week of its release because everyone wants to see themselves in a music video and everyone wants to feel like they're a part of something.

So, here's my thing: the song is kak, but has relatable content. It's radio friendly and comes from the anomaly of young black dudes with instruments making alternative-sounding music, with a great viral music video campaign to boot. It's so great to see people celebrating a bunch of guys who grew up with swimming pools, currently doing blackstrokes in white privilege.

Not that this review will do anything to stop the vomit-worthy worship over its success. I give it a rotten fish head freshly laid by a cat's asshole out of five. Not that anyone gives a shit. This is just another win for capitalism and internet keyboard activists without the brains to even consider something before shitting on it and then turning it into the flavour of the month. The song is for and about you and your world of meta pop cultural irony.

You dumb idiots.

Incensed by the article, he immediately opened his WhatsApp and shared it to the TCCoH group. Jerry replied that they had all read it, together with an emoji of laughing until you cry. In this instance, Xolani was irritated by the emoji and Jerry's happy-go-lucky character.

X: WTF bro?! Who is this kid?!

Ndumo: Some Cape Town hipster white boy.

Jerry: He was probably doing lines with his chick when she played our song in his car.

X: This is bullshit!

Ndumo: **Jerry** 'He was probably doing lines with his chick …' – ahahaha, maybe she's in the music video!

JT: You naais are mal! Lol

X: Guys what the fuck?! This is a shit review.

> We should be taking this thing seriously!!!

> Jerry: **Ndumo** 'ahahaha, maybe she's in the music video!' – we should find her and just post the clip of her dancing to the song on the Insta page hahahaha.

> Ndumo: ahahaha! I vote yes!

> JT: That would be kak funny!

Exasperated with being ignored, Xolani lay back on the grass, popped in his earphones and put a cigarette into his mouth but didn't light it. He stared at the cloudless sky and felt dizzy from going online. Maybe he needed to chill like the other guys, but he was angry about the review. He felt like it was more of a personal attack than a music review. He imagined what his uncle would think of the review, which didn't help things. He could see his phantom father taunting him for trying to make a career out of something that did not have any substance.

The scent of the grass transported him to the garden at home, where he used to sit with Uncle Zweli, being taught the ways of his Xhosa heritage and what would be expected of him when it was time for him to embark on the journey to manhood.

Xolani's love for music and singing came from those sessions. He learnt to sing traditional songs, with his uncle playing the role of conductor in the way he expected his nephew to sing the songs he was teaching him. Uncle Zweli also taught him words from the language and insisted on speaking isiXhosa to him as they sat together.

'Do you want to be a man?' Uncle Zweli would ask, dragging on his cigarette. The acrid smell of its burning contents mixed with the smell of the grass. Xolani would nod at this prompt and Uncle Zweli would be irritated by his soft and shy silence and say, 'Kwedini, what's wrong with you? Use your words.'

'Ewe malume, I want to be a man,' Xolani would tell him softly.

'Speak up!' he'd demand. The more he smoked, the redder his eyes became and Xolani would notice the corners of his mouth beginning to amass a white substance. He knew that soon Uncle Zweli would be speaking more to himself than to him. All he was expected to do was to allow his uncle to speak in a tongue he barely understood, punctuated with small English phrases distorted into sounds resembling the language he spoke.

He pushed away the memories and tried to come back to the moment, taking deep breaths. Immediately, he returned to his irritation at the article. The guy wasn't even writing about their music, he was just trying to embarrass them. Again Xolani tried to move away from negative ruminations, this time by concentrating on the violin's swaying melodies in his earphones. They guided him into another dream of nearly forgotten memories, made up of the night before the morning after. Dancing on stage, singing at the top of his lungs while the microphone dangled limply from his hand, the roar of the crowd, the compliments afterwards.

Closing his eyes, he saw and heard Jerry screaming 'We're doing it!' The tequila shot. The taste.

'I'm willing!' one of Nthabiseng's friends shouted into his ear on the dance floor with her arms around his neck.

'Willing to do what?' he screamed back into her ear, confused.

'Willing to take it as far as you want me to!'

He laughed, and she stormed off.

Chuckling to himself, he tried to piece together getting back to Bell's place. How did he get back here? Wandi? Yes, he vaguely recalled Wandi's voice telling him to 'Get the fuck out the car'. Ringing the buzzer, staggering into Bell's room, her helping him out of his clothes. *Shit. It's barely been a month and I'm already fucking up,* he thought.

He felt a shadow block out the sun and the unlit cigarette being pulled out of his mouth. An insignificant piece of skin on his lower lip was ripped away with it. Before he had a chance to respond to the sting, he felt lips press against his and hair tickling his ears. When she lifted her head, he found himself staring at the cleanest nostrils he had ever seen. He expressed the thought and received a slap to his bare chest for it. She said something that he missed, having been too slow to take out his earphones.

'I'm surprised you're still kissing me after I was such a mess last night,' he said.

'You were fine. I found your closed performance funny, actually. Stumbling over your clothes and all.' Bell giggled.

He sat up to rest his head on his forearm, hiding his face, and mumbled, 'That bad huh?'

'That entertaining.'

He raised an eye to look at her next to him and caught the spark in her hazel eyes that always made her seem excited; short brown hair covering one eye. Strands whispered softly with the passing breeze.

'So, wild show huh?'

'Huh?' he was confused by the sudden question she directed at him.

'That's all you could say about it last night.' She imitated his voice with gestures and the fear of the mess he had been the night before was confirmed.

'Wild. Oh my God so wild. Oh My God that shit was wild! It was wild. Wild. Wil ...' she dramatically dropped her body onto the grass. 'And you passed out,' she finished, shutting her eyes. He tried to hide his face again, but she got up, moved his arm and pressed him back down onto the grass so she could rest her hand and head on his chest.

'So, how's the hangover?' she asked, tickling his chest.

'It's not. I'm still drunk.'

'Oh boy. That means you're going to feel like shit the rest of the day.'

'Yep! Which is perfect. Especially cause I've got studio in, like, an hour. What time is it?'

'It's eleven and you owe me brunch and at least two hours at the market.'

'Hmm …' He began weighing up what she'd just told him. He knew that she was using last night's antics against him.

'There's nothing to think about. You know you're in debt,' she added, as if reading his thoughts.

'Can we meet after studio, though? I'll be done by two-thirty. We just refining the single for radio. Not much to be done, I think JT's pretty much got it on lock. So it's a listening session, really.'

Bell squinted at him with a pressed smile. 'Fine. Three o'clock and you can't be late.'

'Cool, I won't be late.' He suddenly remembered, 'Oh yeah, shit, I almost walked in on Nadia showering this morning.'

'Well that could have been awkward. I can just imagine the speech I would've gotten.'

'What would that have been?'

She started speaking in a high-pitched monotone and put on an Afrikaans accent.

'Bellie, I know that you have not accepted the Lord into your life and that's okay. It's your choice. I really don't mind that Kolani can stays over, but please tell him to at least try to be decent. This morning he just walked into the bathrooms while I was showering, and I really don't like that. I pay rent here and he doesn't; he can't just walk around here like it's his mother's house, just opening doors and no knocking. I know he is your boyfriend en al, but please, you must tell him dat hy moet meer sensitive wees to the fact that jy met iemand saambly.'

'Jeez! Who are you and what have you done with my girlfriend? Really, is that what you put up with? How the hell do you do it?' Xolani exclaimed.

'Don't worry about how I get on with my flatmate. Get your shit together while I go take a shower.'

'Did you see this?' he asked her, while scrolling his phone to the article that had just been posted.

He watched her read it with intermittent gasps and chuckles.

'Yoh, someone's angry!' she remarked when she finished.

'Yeah, and all the guys aren't taking it seriously,' he said, voicing his frustrations.

'Good. Neither should you,' she laughed. 'But that was so rude. Wow!'

He couldn't summon the energy to explain why he felt that he and those closest to him should feel justified anger at the venom and sighed. She pecked his lips and pushed herself up onto her feet using his chest and stomach.

'Aww!' he breathed out.

'Don't be a baby!' she remarked.

He sat up and watched her walk back into the flat. Her nightdress hugged her frame, revealing tanned legs from just where her thighs began. As she reached the glass door she turned around.

'Stop perving!' she shouted, while trying to suppress a smile.

'Wait, did we have sex last night?' he asked her.

She laughed. 'Do you think there was any chance you could have had sex with *anyone* in the state you were in?'

'Then why were my boxers off?'

'The answer to that question lies within you!' she replied cryptically before disappearing behind the sliding door.

He saw himself in the reflection and mouthed, 'Screw this up and it's official Xolani, you're a fucking idiot!'

Bell popped her head back out the door. She asked if she could leave her car at his parents' house. He tilted his head as she blew him a kiss and vanished. He smiled, slowly got up and made his way to her room, moving at a slug's pace.

\*

They hopped off the taxi and made their way towards the popular Sammy Marks Square. Thami had convinced Nthabiseng to start off at the street cypher, before they made their way to the real adventure. A tall and lanky figure, Thami always dressed with the intention of being a nondescript observer in any room. His clothes were simple and never branded. A pair of takkies, a plain white T-shirt and a pair of loosely fitting beige jeans.

As they walked past the market towards the State Theatre, Nthabiseng became a site of attention from vendors and passers-by alike. A few wolf-whistles and heckles about her light skin, or pointed questions about whether or not she was coloured. Others simply yelled 'Lekgoa' at her. She acted as if she couldn't hear them.

'You outchea handling town like a local,' Thami remarked.

'Nothing men scream at you in the streets is imaginative enough to change, wherever you are. I also wouldn't mind if you didn't talk down to me.' She peered at him sideways.

'I just meant that, like, I mean, you obviously know how to handle or take care of yourself. I just meant, like … you know,' he said. 'We're, like, in a place that you probably don't usually come to. I mean, I can't imagine that you're a city-centre regular, is what I'm trying to say.'

She kept quiet and concentrated her gaze on the ground as they walked to the place where all the action was said to be. She wore a long green, black and white skirt with swirling patterns that danced just above her ankles. The bright white tips of her Converse takkies made their blue material seem to glisten with novelty. The yellow T-shirt that hugged her arms and loosened up at the torso made her a visible sunflower in the city square. As the view of the State Theatre became larger on approach, so too did the group of rappers formed in several circles dubbed 'cyphers'. Some clocked Thami's approach and began to shout and whistle at him. On his and Nthabiseng's arrival, a few of the guys taking part in the cyphers came to greet him.

This was an unusual sight for Nthabiseng. She'd never really seen Thami interact with many people; he mostly kept to himself at school. Every now and then she'd see him speaking to the stoners, wannabe rappers and some of the other strange kids that no one could really figure out. But none of them seemed to be friendships. He always looked like he was just in polite conversation.

'Damn Thami, you on that Cashless Society "Hottentot Hop"?' someone called out to him. It was one of the older guys from the cypher who was considered a bit of a legend in these parts. Thami recognised that he was trying to push his buttons both by testing his music knowledge and insulting Nthabiseng's mixed race. The guy's name was Rele, a.k.a. Rebel-One, one of the older hip-hop heads who resented the likes of Thami and his peers. They saw the youngsters as a new breed of spoilt kids who'd never understand how hard they needed to fight to earn their places in the community. They snarled at them for being of a time when internet connections allowed them to download as much music as they wanted to on their phones. While they, the elders, had come from having to first prove their knowledge to the gatekeepers of their day, before being allowed to hear whatever new material they were able to get their hands on, then wait their turn for a single copy CD to make its way through multiple hands in the city before landing in their hifi systems.

The others around Rebel-One laughed and shoved him. Thami smiled and shook his head at him.

'Rebel, why you gotta be like that, though? You know "I'm always hunting with the spear of the nation, called a AK",' Thami quipped back a line from the old classic Rebel-One had referenced. Nthabiseng missed the interaction altogether, still consumed by the new-forming image of her schoolmate. The guys greeting Thami started to introduce themselves to Nthabiseng. They were a motley crew of clashing styles, signifying their tastes and the eras of the music they affiliated themselves with. The place was mostly filled with the new-school rappers that Rebel-One associated with

Thami's generation. They donned skinny jeans and Vans sneakers for the most part. They had nose rings and other jewellery studding their faces and the ones who kept abreast of trends shaved the sides of their heads, allowing the dreads or single plaits atop their heads to flop over. Others, who still considered themselves followers of the 'old-school' era of hip-hop called her 'sister' and 'queen' and wore head wraps and all sorts of Rastafari paraphernalia. The rest of them were still in their school uniforms; shirts undone, roughed-up afros, ties hanging to the side and pants hanging below their asses. Around them the sound of people making percussive beats with their mouths was ubiquitous. So too was the sound of various rap battles, with the crowds huddled around each rapper or crew exclaiming a protracted 'Yoh!' every time someone dropped a punchline that they appreciated. The smell of weed was thick in the air and one of the guys offered Nthabiseng a hit. She looked at Thami, who looked back and shrugged his shoulders.

    She enjoyed the state of being high and thought that she might miss out on a special element of the situation without a little aid. The blunt was smooth on her throat and felt fluffy when she released. The amount of smoke she blew out took her by surprise. After a few drags, she thanked the person who'd been kind enough to share and handed it back to him. He smiled at her and then turned to Thami.

'Eksê, Thami!' he called suddenly. 'How come you didn't put me on the clip last week? Come on, joh! You know I can win this thing! Ska ba so!'

Thami smiled sheepishly at him, 'Eish bra, harde. You know YFM is super strict about me keeping the videos to two minutes. Also, you can't be rapping scripts if you want to get a shot at the freestyle competition.'

He smiled, and a few others started laughing at the guy he had been speaking to.

'Ah! Die blah! Kgante ke eng? When have I ever busted a script at the cypher?' he asked Thami, injured by the accusation.

'Every cat here saw your rhyme book, nigga! You were rapping holding it behind your back! Anyway, we all know your punchlines by heart now,' someone else jumped in. There was more laughter at the guy's expense; he just wanted a chance. Nthabiseng stood around and laughed lazily at the events unfolding in front of her.

'Hey,' a soft voice spoke from behind her. As she turned around to look, the source walked around to face her, confusing her movements. When Nthabiseng finally steadied her vision, she saw a young woman wearing an African-print dress, head wrap and beads around her neck and wrists. She also wore thick, black, round spectacle frames that enlarged her surprisingly green eyes.

Nthabiseng returned a lazy 'Hey' to her.

'You don't remember me, do you?' the stranger smiled curiously. Nthabiseng rummaged through her memories, trying to place the woman. She took her time looking at her, but her mind couldn't help but paint the image of her face onto an unrelated character. A character conjured from the recesses of Nthabiseng's incoherence of thoughts and feelings, but one that simultaneously remained whoever she actually was, the person standing in front of her. Eventually, she had to tell the enigmatic figure the truth.

'I'm sorry, I don't. I'm sorry,' she said, blushing slightly.

'Don't worry about it,' the stranger returned with a warm smile. She suddenly became a real person again, no longer the character Nthabiseng had been imagining. 'I'm Tsholo. I was in your brother's year. It's crazy to see you now.'

'Wait ... I kind of remember you. You were a bit of a rebel from the Mams crew, if I remember correctly,' Nthabiseng told her, taking her time to pronounce each word.

'I was indeed. It's cool to see you out here. Did you come with Thami?' she asked.

'Yeah, I did,' Nthabiseng replied. She paused for a second, then asked, 'How come he has friends?'

Tsholo laughed, and Nthabiseng realised that what she had said did not land as intended.

'I mean ...' she started, as Tsholo lit a joint of her

own, 'I mean, he never talks to anyone at school. So, it's kind of weird to see so many people, like ... happy to see him, you know what I mean?'

Tsholo's eyes began to close slightly as she dragged on her joint and listened to Nthabiseng. 'It makes sense that Thami would bring you here now.'

Nthabiseng looked at her, waiting for her to say more. Tsholo passed the joint to Nthabiseng, who took it. She then motioned with her head and led her to a bench closer to the action.

'Why do you think all these kids are here?'

Nthabiseng shrugged as she passed the joint back. She felt her thoughts begin to speed up and got the feeling that she was about to be told something profound.

Tsholo looked at her and smiled mysteriously. She then turned her focus to the cypher in front of her as Nthabiseng followed her gaze. From where they were sitting, they could peer into the circle where the kids were going at it passionately. She listened to the guy currently rapping in front of her. He was in direct confrontation with another dude in front of him, while the others bobbed their heads to the rhythm of the beatbox and listened closely, waiting for the next punchline that would give him a one-up on his opponent.

'You're in an outdated class like a top hat, that makes your style a fashionable sin like your clothing mismatch!' he spat at his challenger and the crowd erupted into cheers and laughter, indicating their approval. Nthabiseng noticed that Thami was standing on a bench opposite them, with his camera pointed at the performance. He was entirely focused on catching the moment. The other rapper jumped in to get his own back.

'Are you performing for him?' he pointed at Thami's camera. 'You trying to get on YFM, but you don't realise, you have less class than a bottle of Gordon's gin!' The crowd erupted again, several of them slapping him on the shoulder for his clapback. Nthabiseng looked at Tsholo, who, she noticed, had been smiling at her the entire time.

'Thami takes videos of the legendary cyphers here and posts them on his blog. Some intern at YFM happened across them when one of his friends posted a link on Facebook. They figured it would be the best way to discover rappers from Pretoria and decided to commission Thami for his videos. None of them get deals out of it, of course,' Tsholo said, looking at the crowd. 'But every now and then, a well-known rapper decides to feature them on one of their tracks, then it's up to them to make whatever they can of the opportunity.'

Nthabiseng looked at the cypher and then back at Thami.

'So, you see, school isn't where others decide to live their lives,' Tsholo said.

Nthabiseng looked at Tsholo and shared a coy smile.

'Of course, you would know this. How's your brother by the way?' Tsholo asked.

'Apparently, he's on his way to being a superstar,' Nthabiseng shared impatiently.

'I guess that question must be getting a little irritating.' Tsholo chuckled to herself. 'You know, that guy ... we could never really figure him out in school either. He was so weird, but we just thought it was because he was an art student. Then, one day we see him on stage at a talent show, with Ndumo and Jerry who suddenly looked like they also hated combing their hair as much as he did. It's weird – they weren't like that in primary school. I mean, Ndumo and Jerry used to play in the band at our church in Mamelodi. So, when Xolani pitched up it was surprising how quickly they changed.' They both chuckled. 'I won't lie, we didn't get it at all. It just sounded like a bunch of noise, but we liked that the lyrics were in vernac. Other than that, we just spent our time laughing at them and their weird music.' She laughed, shook her head and smiled to herself. Nthabiseng thought about her brother in high school.

'Hey!' Thami said, suddenly standing in front of them and bringing both back from wherever they had travelled to in their heads.

'Hey,' Nthabiseng smiled.

Tsholo got up and hugged him. 'Hey baby boy, how're you?'

'I'm good. Aren't you going to show these kids how it's done today?' he asked Tsholo. She laughed.

'Not today, I haven't heard a punchline worthy of my energy and I need real peers if I'm even going to get a proper warm-up,' she quipped. 'Anyway, I've been keeping Nthabiseng company while you were off securing your next e-wallet payment.'

He laughed.

'We're probably going to head to Marabastad. I've got enough footage here to work with; C4 blew up the spot again. Y'all gonna start taking him seriously soon.' He smiled at her. Tsholo eyed him curiously.

'Marabastad?' she asked, looking at Thami first and then Nthabiseng.

'Yeah, we figured we'd probably get some interesting photos and footage there. Especially as night falls,' he told her.

She remained silent for a while, contemplating the pair.

'What interesting footage and pics are you expecting to get from there?' she asked patiently.

'The other side of the city, I guess,' Nthabiseng replied. 'We're living this sheltered life and we reckon we might as well explore the other side of the curtain and reflect on how that's not all there is to Pretoria,' she told Tsholo solemnly. Tsholo continued to look at them with a contemplative gaze.

'Why?' she finally asked.

Thami laughed nervously. 'Hawu! Did she not just explain our *why*?'

Tsholo went quiet for a time, looking in front of her. Thami looked at Nthabiseng, who looked back at him with bloodshot eyes. She shrugged to indicate her own confusion. She was about to get up when Tsholo finally spoke again, forcing her to remain seated.

'Do you guys ever watch soccer?' She let the question hang in the air, before she continued, 'I always find watching South African soccer a bit of a rollercoaster. But I also love the fact that we have such loyal fans here.' She abruptly turned to them and asked, 'And do you guys ever watch South African soccer?'

They looked at each other, then back at her and shrugged.

'You know, what's interesting about us is that most soccer fans we know have a team they support here, but they are often more invested in English teams. It makes sense, I guess, cause while it's cool to watch players dribble and work the ball, the entire aim of the game is to score goals, right?' she paused. 'The problem with the South African PSL is that we never really see anyone scoring goals. Apparently, the Orlando Pirates coach once said that he had travelled the planet but had never seen players more incapable of scoring goals than here. The guy thinks that for some reason our psychology in South Africa won't allow us to put balls in the back of the net.' She chuckled and so did they.

They listened intently as she continued, 'Imagine your coach not just dissing your team alone for losing, but the entire country you play for!' They continued to laugh. 'It sounds like this guy would prefer that our teams scored own goals just to prove that we understand the relationship between the ball, the net and the game's aim. Or our lack of it, in this case.' She paused and smiled at them, closely watching their expressions as she spoke. 'But do you know why our players don't score own goals, even if it would bring more excitement to the game?'

Nthabiseng and Thami were hanging on to her every word.

'Because they understand that no matter how hard it is for them to score goals against the other team, that is the minimum they are required to do in a game. Scoring own goals would equate to admitting that they defeat themselves as a team, which would show their fans that they have absolutely no respect for them or themselves.' She looked at them. Both seemed to be lost as to what she was trying to tell them.

'You see, more than any other sport, soccer is comprised of regional communities. That's why, more often than not, you'll see two or more teams coming from the same place. Johannesburg alone has six teams. What do you think that means?'

'That people are proud of where they come from?' Nthabiseng offered a non-committal response.

'So it's probably not the best idea then, to go around antagonising those fans by waving the flag of the other team or hood, right?' Tsholo asked.

'Probably not, I guess,' Thami said.

'It's getting a bit dark. It's probably the perfect time to take your camera home,' she told Thami. She got up, hugged Nthabiseng and told her to greet her brother. She shared a final sardonic smile with them and joined the growing circle in front of them. The orange glow from the lights outside the theatre was becoming more pronounced. They shared a smile with each other and caught a taxi back to the mall where Thami had parked his car.

*

"Then I see this guy swaying on the dance floor drunk out of his mind! And some little girl whispering in his ear!'

The room erupted with laughter.

'Wait ... wait ... then she puts her arms around his neck, says something to him and this fool laughs at her!' he continued.

The howling laughter filled the room once again, reaching noise levels high enough to disrupt the eardrum. Xolani was sprawled across the three-seater sofa, hitting his hand on the floor and burying his face in the arm rest. Jerry was bent over, holding his stomach, jumping up and down to express the agony caused by the laughter; his regularly low voice transformed into a high-pitched cackle. JT sat in a corner behind the mixing desk and smiled at the room. Ndumo was crawling in circles on the carpet, gasping for breath, tears streaming down his face.

'Hawu! What was I supposed to do? She goes to school with my little sister!' Xolani exclaimed.

'No, wait. What I wanna know ... is what that girl ... said to you,' Ndumo shouted in between coughs from the floor. He rolled around, struggling to control his laughter. A sneer slowly crossed his face. His big, lazy eyes concentrated on Xolani. Ndumo's afro cushioned his head as he relaxed on the studio's carpet. He pulled a cigarette out of the box in the pocket of his low-hanging jeans. He put it in his mouth and struck a match. Xolani sat up on the couch, resting his head on the sofa's backrest. He also reached for his cigarette box but found it empty.

'Skyf,' he called to Ndumo. Ndumo threw his box, which Xolani caught with one hand against his chest. After tossing the box aside he took a lighter out of his pocket and lit the cigarette on the second click. He dropped the lighter on the couch. He felt a sluggish pain coming over his body and an irritability rising within him. The hangover was kicking in and he wasn't keen on Ndumo's knack to spark a constant ribbing at his expense. To get his own back, Xolani played into a moment of silence and took his time to respond.

'Khuluma ndoda, sifun'ukwazi!' Ndumo shouted at him.

Xolani began a routine that they were all too familiar with. It was described as 'X's performance'. It was the thing that made him such an endearing performer. The enigmatic ability to hold a secret from an audience yet alert them to the fact that they needed to know what it was, thus making them hunger for more while he gave them nothing. It started with his head bowed, the top visible as his dreads formed a veil over his face. Then the cigarette disappeared behind the veil and his hand emerged empty.

'Hey! We're not your fucking groupies! Hurry up and tell us the story so that we can get back to finishing our work!' JT had a way of controlling everyone when they let things go too far. Being the eldest in the group, it didn't really surprise anyone. Behind the spectacles was a short, stout man with a balding head.

Xolani snapped out of his trance and whined in a high-pitched voice. 'JT, why you always gotta kill my buzz?' He lifted his shoulders and dropped his hands.

'Cause your buzz is killing *me*! Now, what did that little chick say?'

Xolani sucked on his teeth to express his disapproval. 'Whatever, man,' he said, clearly deflated. 'She was just like "I'm willing."'

The room went quiet, everybody holding in their laughter, anticipating the punchline on its way. 'And I was like, "Willing to do what?" And she was like, "*Willing to take it as far as you want to take it.*" That's when I laughed at her ...'

The room remained silent except for a few awkward chuckles from Jerry. JT and Ndumo quietly looked at each other and shook their heads.

'So, Xolani tell us again ...' Ndumo started. 'Why didn't you do big things with this girl?'

Jerry protested through nervous giggles on Xolani's behalf, 'The man is recently married, guy!'

'Since when is that an excuse?' Ndumo asked. He got up to put out his cigarette at the ashtray on the desk. He leaned his backside on the mixing desk next to JT. His baby-blue skinnies made Xolani think of a smurf. Then Ndumo crossed his arms and focused his giant spheres on Xolani.

'Truthfully, what I really wanna know is whether the model older brother is indeed living the life that he projects to his little sister. Or if he's fallen off the wagon.'

JT stood up next to Ndumo and he too crossed his arms and stared at Xolani with the hostile look that preceded merciless banter.

'Dude, I'm not into cradle snatching. So, if you're hoping for a chance with her and asking for my blessing, then go for it. What I'm concerned about is what the fuck we're going to do about this shitting turd Donald Sterling. We can't let this shit just fucking fly like it's cool,' Xolani said.

Ndumo scoffed, 'So, what do you suggest we do, big boy?'

Xolani felt himself getting increasingly frustrated at the casual response from Ndumo and didn't understand why no one else felt the injury of the write-up. Was it because he had written the song and they didn't appreciate its significance?

'X,' JT began, 'have you never heard the expression "There's no such thing as bad publicity"? Have you seen how many more views that article has gotten the song? Why are you taking this so personally, bra? It's perfect! In fact, I think we should hope this idiot writes more about us!'

'Really, it's nothing to worry about, man,' Jerry told Xolani, patting him on the back.

'Personally, I love our racist fans the most!' Ndumo declared smugly to laughter in the room. He registered that Xolani was still frustrated and nonchalantly added, 'Bra, this guy is trying to make us feel guilty for being black and you're letting him win. He'll conveniently forget that part when he meets us at some point and tries to suck our dicks for tickets. Chill.'

'Exactly!' Jerry and JT echoed.

Xolani nodded and felt slightly reassured that they understood where he was coming from. He was still irritated that it took Ndumo to acknowledge his feelings, for the others to listen. He dismissed his touchiness, attributing it to his hangover, and suppressed the growing resentment he felt, given that he was the founding band member.

*

Bell and Xolani made their way through the Hatfield market hosted in the mall's parking lot. His cap and sunglasses couldn't protect him from the sun's glare and he still found himself squinting. He was clumsily following Bell through the crowd of people, most of whom were haggling with the vendors to get cheaper prices for the already dirt-cheap products on offer. He had an unfriendly exchange with the incense that tickled his nose. The sweet scent was overbearing and gave him the feeling of being strangled and punched in the gut. The heat didn't help. He felt his sweat glands in overdrive and was disorientated by the racket made by the crowd. Bell looked back at him to share a smile, which he reluctantly returned. She took his hand in hers and led him through the mass of people. He was uncomfortable with this display, which earned them disapproving looks from all the market attendants. It made Xolani more anxious in his hungover state.

He suspected that Bell was oblivious to the public's intrusions.

The only time she seemed to notice was after a few drinks and then she would become confrontational. They'd swap roles and he'd be the one pleading with her to ignore them. She once got them into a physical face-off in a club; the incident didn't earn him much respect. Bell had felt disrespected by another woman who had been giving them disdainful looks. She had felt that the woman had been staring at the two of them for far too long and took umbrage. Xolani spent the better part of the evening trying to convince Bell of the futility of getting into a confrontation with the other woman. He tried to convince her that any aggression directed at the other party wouldn't help the situation. At some point that night, Bell found herself sharing the dance floor with the woman and took the opportunity to shove her because she felt that she had invaded her space. This sparked a contest between the two women. One of the woman's male friends located Xolani at the bar on the club's balcony.

'Hey, monna! Come take care of your fucking white girl!' he shouted at him. Xolani had just taken a shot and simply gave the man a blank stare.

'I said, go handle lekgoa la hao! Jou fokken snaai!' he shouted as he advanced on Xolani and pushed him into the bar counter, not giving a thought to the other bodies in the queue who were forced to jump out of his path. Still stupefied by the chain of events taking place, Xolani found himself taking a punch to the face before he registered that he was in a fight. He staggered to one side and grabbed onto the balcony's railing. As the man prepared to take another swing at him, Xolani grabbed a beer off the bar counter and threw it into his assailant's face in the desperate hope that it would slow him down. The punch still flew through the air but landed on his shoulder. Xolani began to swing his arms in a wild windmill motion, hoping to land a good blow at some point, employing the logic of volume and passion over technique.

He couldn't be sure if his shots were hitting his intended target as he swung with eyes tightly shut. Instead, he found himself in a bear hug. When he opened his eyes, he realised that one of the club's bouncers, Frederico, was swiftly carrying him to the opposite side of the balcony. He hadn't even noticed that he had been lifted off his feet until he looked into his saviour's face. The barman was shouting at the other bouncer, Andrew, that he had the culprit who started the fight in his vice grip. The drama that had started on the dance floor had spilled out onto the balcony and, somehow, had worked out in favour of Bell and Xolani. As regular patrons of the club, and because Xolani often played there, the manager immediately took their side. He kicked the other woman and her friends out of the club. Their protestations of racism were drowned out by the music. Frederico had dropped Xolani and sat him down. He laid a heavy hand on his shoulder. Out of breath and wild-eyed, Xolani looked back at the bar to see if his tormentor was still there.

'My man, you need to hire me as your bodyguard because you cannot fight,' Frederico laughed at him. Bell ran to Xolani on the balcony, asking if he was okay. He looked at her in shock, still out of breath. He had not yet figured out what had just happened. Frederico told her that he was fine and that she needed a boyfriend who could fight and protect her. His eyebrow had swollen up a little bit. They definitely needed more drinks before they left the club that night.

The next morning, Bell told him the real version of the events that had taken place the night before. She cried and apologised profusely for her antics. She tried to spoil him that day with all kinds of things she could pay for and he made an effort to tell her it wasn't necessary. Instead, he attempted to comfort her and told her that it was just a night when she was being a bad drunk and it could happen to anyone. However, he couldn't shake the guilt he felt; he knew that something unjust had happened but couldn't articulate it to himself, least of all to her. There was a fragility in their relationship that he wasn't ready to test. He felt that they both felt a need to overcompensate, but he couldn't say why.

He was jolted back to the market by Bell calling his name as they stood in front of a Rasta selling Bob Marley regalia.

'Hey!' she waved a hand in front of his face, bringing him back from his daze. He blinked a few times behind his sunglasses, cocked his head to the side and smiled to show he was registering her presence.

'Hi,' he rasped, then cleared his throat. 'Sorry, I'm here! What's up?'

'What do you think of this?' She held up a small brown pouch, with red, yellow and green stripes on it. He raised an eyebrow at her, before he realised that she was serious about buying it.

'I give you nice price, sista. You see, you keep nice small tingz in dis bag,' the Rasta called out. 'Jah Rastafari,' he greeted Xolani. The Rasta's dreadlocks were thick and closing in on his waist. Given a minute or two they could have been counted. He played reggae from his stall, most of the lyrics unintelligible to Xolani's and Bell's untrained ears. Under the watchful eyes of the Rasta, Xolani looked around the stall, noting all the Bob Marley accessories, T-shirts and medallions, which probably made up the bulk of his sales. Rasta wore a medallion of his own, but it had the picture of a light-skinned man dressed in a white military uniform.

Xolani finally smiled and returned, 'Sho faya,' a

phrase he'd picked up to address Rastas. He hoped that it was being deployed in the correct context. He felt the impulse to shake his dreads in his address, to which the Rasta smiled and shook his own too. He turned back to Bell who giggled at the exchange.

'Sure, it looks pretty cool,' she said to Rasta. She offered him the asking price; he clasped the cash with both hands and balled them into two fists that he pulled to his chest.

'We give tanks, sista. And here for you, brotha. No charge.' He handed Xolani a black plastic ring embroidered with the same colours as the pouch Bell had just purchased.

'Thank you, my brother,' Xolani accepted with a mimicked grace the Rasta had offered earlier. The Rasta thanked them again with his two fists held together, rocking them in the air just in front of his face, slightly swaying on the spot. As they walked away waving with their heads turned, they bumped into another couple who also hadn't been watching where they walked. As they all began to mutter apologies, Xolani and the other man recognised one another.

'X!' yelled the man and pulled him into an embrace.

'Anton!' Xolani exclaimed. 'Yoh!' They stood apart for a moment to take each other in.

'It's fucking good to see you, chana!'

Anton was a heavyset bald guy. He was about a head taller than Xolani, his wiry frame an exact six feet, with tanned and freckled skin. His smile was wide enough to reach his cheek bones and he had bulging eyes that made him look constantly frightened.

'I'm great man! How are you doing?' Xolani asked.

'Ag, good my bra!' Anton replied.

Xolani felt Bell squeeze his hand.

'Oh, shit!' he said. 'This is my girlfriend, Bell,' he said gesturing to her.

'Ag, jammer my skat! How are you? I'm Anton.' Anton stretched out his hand and Bell took it.

'I know! It's great to finally meet you; the song you guys did together always brings me to tears,' she told Anton.

'Ag, dankie!' he blushed slightly. 'And this is my liefie, Marie-Anne.'

Bell and Xolani took turns to shake hands with Marie-Anne.

'Aangename kennis,' she said.

Anton invited them to a late lunch, an invitation that was accepted. They settled on the News Cafe down the road and sat outside to enjoy the weather. They took seats on a ledge that looked out on Hatfield's Burnett Street, near the entrance of the notorious Hatfield Square.

The Square was a coming-of-age location for the youth of Pretoria. Primarily dominated by Afrikaner students and rugby zealots, it was rare to visit the site without witnessing a punch-up, charged by triple

Klippies and cola specials, testosterone and, often, steroids. Racial clashes were commonplace. In these instances, security – without fail – would beat and eject the black participants in any given fight. If anyone had ventured into the Square without hearing the term 'kaffir' casually or aggressively thrown around, they had probably been walking with their ears closed. Nevertheless, the area was the closest thing to a cosmopolitan enclave the city had. The many teenagers who'd grown up in integrated spaces had become an insurmountable force that the stubborn city of Pretoria could not fight. Every year the demographics became ever more mercurial for the old guard. They were forced to concede defeat to a new generation that was taking their place. The bouncers at club entrances seemingly changed overnight from blond-haired, red-faced Afrikaners to African foreign nationals in black leather blazers, who at the very least, acknowledged the value of money from the black youth at their doors.

Anton ordered the table a round of cocktails and everyone placed their meal orders at the same time.

'So, Marie-Anne, what do you do?' Bell initiated small talk with Anton's girlfriend. The table listened to the tale of mousy Marie-Anne's quest to become a nurse. She had been inspired by her grandmother and her innate character to always take care of people. Next to Anton, Marie-Anne was a tiny figure. Anton listened to her intently, as if he were hearing her story for the first time. He punctuated her story with an 'Ag, my skat' or a 'Liefie' here and there, staring at her adoringly.

Anton was complete in his chivalry. At the door of the restaurant he had stood waiting for the women to enter first. He had pulled Marie-Anne's chair out when they got to the table, before taking his own seat. A few strands of Marie-Anne's sandy blonde hair fell onto her face; Anton beat her to returning the strands to behind her ear.

'Dankie skat.' Her tiny, pointed nose flushed slightly pink and she smiled sweetly at her boyfriend.

'Dis 'n plesier liefie,' he said to her, flashing his diminutive teeth.

'You guys are absolutely adorable!' Bell said. 'How long have you been together?' she asked, as the waiter brought their drinks. Anton insisted that they clink glasses and make eye contact.

After everyone had their first sips, Marie-Anne responded, 'Eight years.' She blushed. Anton shared her blush.

'Wow!' Xolani exclaimed. The cocktail made his hangover a little more bearable. 'Wait ... that means ...' he started counting on his fingers, 'that you guys have been together since you started high school.'

'Ja ...' Anton smiled bashfully. 'Well I was in Grade 10 when she was in Grade 8. But ja.' He smiled with pride. Two waiters arrived at the table to drop off their meals.

'Let's eat!' Xolani announced.

## KNOWLEDGE

*The generations had yielded results beyond ordinary marvel. The Fish retained an eye for detail that The Children missed in their pious dedications to the land and equal exchange. Their service to memory was not synced to that of The Fish. The Children assumed that The Fish were predisposed to an amiable, observatory manner. Although The Children had taught them the ways of the land – where speech was performed without bubbles – they remained an inexplicable presence. Their assimilation retained an incomplete inference. It was often pointed out that their tongues were the only muscles that had not adapted to their new lives on land. They all concurred that it was the size and strength of this important and inconspicuous organ that they needed to help the newcomers develop.*

*The Children decided that the best way to aid the process of allowing The Fish the full privileges of an amphibious existence was for them to marry into the indigenous keepers of the land. So it came to pass that the next generation was comprised of Childish Fish that walked on land as well as they swam in the sea. Their*

tongues were big and strong enough to allow them the versatility of a dual existence, but with the limited memories of The Fish. The Children took this as confirmation that their knowledge was in tune with the nature of the world's land and sea. Soon, the land was covered by The Children, their Childish Fish, as well as The Fish that had first sought out land but remained adapted rather than assimilated.

In this harmony it was decided that it was time the scales of water and land be balanced. It was time The Children be given the opportunity to explore the depths of the ocean with help from The Fish. Agreed and decided upon, the first of The Children, Fish and Childish Fish descended into the ocean in a bubble-like container that was built for The Children and dragged beneath by The Fish. It was not long before The Fish returned for the new groups who waited excitedly to explore the planes below. No Children returned and it was accepted that it was for the same reason that The Fish walked freely on land. Soon it was so that more bubbles were built so droves of excited Children could make their way below. Few remained in the promise to maintain the land and homes. None who left returned. The Childish Fish whose memories, like The Fish, did not rely on the past but on the present, assumed the land as theirs. The few remaining Children were believed to be anomalous to the area. It was decided that in their small numbers, the foreign beings were to *be quarantined, for they seemed to be possessed by a psychosis of memory that The Childish Fish and Fish alike did not suffer from. The Children had, in vain, attempted to remind The Childish Fish and Fish, of how it came to be that they had come to possess the land. To try to confront them with the reality that it was in fact they who were aliens. It was a tale that was dismissed as a groundless assertion by those now in command of the land, who were clearly of both land and sea and, therefore, the earth. The Children were declared mad by both The Childish Fish and The Fish. Their tongues, it was said, were the source of their madness. From time to time, a Childish Fish would suffer from the psychosis of remembering and would be quarantined with the rest of the mad Children. The psychosis of memory subjected its victims to speaking in tongues. A vernacular denied and forgotten.*

\*

Nthabiseng was sitting on her balcony staring out at her view of Pretoria. The house sat on the top of a koppie that gave them a mountain-range-like backyard that loomed over a large portion of Pretoria East, including its notorious Mamelodi township, marked by its lack of a tree line. The disappearance was an interesting, sudden sight in the view from where she sat. She thought about her afternoon with Thami and what Tsholo had said to them. The soccer metaphor had confused her and left her wondering why Tsholo had spoken so cryptically to them. She hadn't seemed taken by their wanting to go to Marabastad and Nthabiseng couldn't understand what the harm would have been. All they wanted to do was discover and show other parts of the city to their circles, which would otherwise never see them. What was Tsholo's deal?

Nthabiseng could feel the effects of the weed wearing off, yet she still felt a little light. She walked into the kitchen craving a snack and the taste of Earl Grey. As she flicked the kettle on, the intercom rang.

'Great! Who the hell could that be?' she said to herself. Not in the mood for company, she remembered telling the others that she didn't feel like going to dinner that night. Looking at the intercom monitor she saw Siya, with Monique next to him, pulling faces into the camera. She pressed the button to open the gate without lifting the receiver. Before turning away, she saw another car pull into the driveway. *Great!* she thought.

'Hello? Is anybody here? We come bearing gifts!' Monique shouted from the entrance. Nthabiseng carried on preparing her tea without calling back.

'Alcohol!' Monique shouted excitedly.

*I know*, Nthabiseng thought. She put her tea bag

into a coffee mug. Siya walked into the kitchen holding a case of ciders on top of a case of beers. Tumi and Monique walked in carrying grocery bags full of food.

'And dinner!' she heard Pieter's voice shout before he turned into the kitchen. Behind him, Jason and Joan walked in. Jason was holding a bottle of brandy in one hand and vodka in the other. They all smiled at Nthabiseng, who simply looked at them with the mug in hand and sighed.

They sat on the balcony with the city lights spread out in front of them. Tumi and Joan had teamed up to make the night's meal. Completely full, Nthabiseng delegated dish-washing duty to Pieter, who protested the unfair treatment. Joan offered to do the job for her boyfriend, but Nthabiseng was resolute in her satisfied and tipsy state that Pieter was to do it, considering that it was his idea for them to gate-crash.

'But I bought all the booze!' he exclaimed.

'Fuck it! I'll take this one for you buddy,' Siya volunteered.

'Now that's a team player!' Pieter happily pounded Siya's fist and rubbed his head. 'This is why you're our captain. A real leader knows when he must serve!' They both chuckled.

'You guys heard that the Sipplatons are coming this year?' Jason broke in.

'You mean the Simpletons?' Monique corrected him. The table erupted in laughter at Jason's expense.

He sank back into the camper chair that he was sitting in.

'Who the fuck cares though? You'd never catch me dead at one of their shows,' Siya told the table.

'If you ever want to have sex in your life again, you will,' Tumi quietly stated, peering at him sideways. They all roared with laughter again.

'Shame, Siya,' Nthabiseng said as she stood up, 'I'm on my way to the bathroom. I think you might have left your balls there; I'll look for them for you.' Her jibe was the nail in the coffin that left Siya completely defeated. Joan got up from her seat to comfort him with a hug. Nthabiseng listened to her friends tittering as she walked down the hall towards her bathroom. As she sat down she pulled out her phone and checked her messages. A voicemail from her brother letting her know that he was going to sleep at his girlfriend's house. Another voicemail, from her mother, who was checking that everything was okay, that they were fine for the weekend and to call if they needed anything. Another message came in while she washed her hands.

> Thami: So I guess Tsholo's a bit of a negative Nelly, huh?

She was glad he had made contact but wasn't in the space to have an entire text conversation. She knew he'd know that the message had been received but figured he could wait a while. She switched her phone to aeroplane mode and sauntered back to her friends with a finger tracing an invisible line on the wall.

*

The double date had become a splendid evening for everyone at the table, with only a few disruptions from Xolani's and Anton's respective fans asking to take pictures with them. A few of them had requested selfies with the two of them together, having heard their bands' freshly released collaboration on SoundCloud. The pair was accommodating of the requests. It was a pleasantly warm Pretoria evening; the heat leaving the cement could be felt as it made its way up into the skies of South Africa's capital. As the cocktails kept coming, Marie-Anne became livelier and more vocal. She extended an invitation to the other couple, to Anton's farm, saying that it would be a lekker weekend just outside of Pretoria.

'Well, the last time we let these two leave Pretoria together, we lost communication with them for a day and they came back with the most beautiful song I've ever heard, so yes! I'm in!' Bell declared. 'But only if they get the same mushrooms …'

'Um, wait, should we get shots?' Xolani suddenly asked loudly. Bell noticed Anton's face going crimson, he was wide eyed and looking at Xolani.

'Yeah, I think a round of Jäger Bombs should be good, right? I mean we're all already over the drinking limit; we'll just leave our cars here and catch a Maxi cab home,' Xolani continued, improvising his diversion. Bell turned to look at Marie-Anne, who had a bemused smile on her face as she looked from Xolani, to Bell and finally, landing her gaze on Anton.

'Mushrooms?' she asked sweetly.

'Shit!' said Anton.

'Shit!' echoed Bell.

'I'm just gonna go find our waiter and get us those Jäger Bombs,' Xolani announced and broke free in search of their waiter. As he entered the restaurant, he almost knocked over the very person he was looking for, betrayed by his hasty departure.

'Harde, bra wa ka!' he offered as an apology.

'No stress, bra. Le grand mo?' the waiter asked.

'Actually, I was going to ask if we could maybe get a round of Jäger Bombs for the table?' he replied.

'Sho, no stress, I'll get them,' the waiter told him.

Xolani proceeded to make his way to the bathroom, where he contemplated the scene playing outside. On his way back he braced himself for the tension. As he was about to turn to their table, he noticed for the first time a stage in the corner, with instruments. *Fuck, I hope there isn't some shitty house band playing here tonight*, he thought to himself.

He arrived to solemn faces looking up at him.

'Fuck,' he sighed as he sat down.

'Kolani,' Marie-Anne started. He wasn't in the mood for this line of inquiry and was ready to call for the bill. She continued, 'The next time you take mushrooms please make sure we're all together.'

The other three burst into laughter around him. He was gobsmacked at what he had just heard.

'What?' he asked. The others carried on laughing.

'How old do you think I am?' Marie-Anne asked. 'I don't know what this one's problem is, thinking I'd be angry!' She punched Anton's shoulder.

'Oh fuck, well, this is a relief,' Xolani said to her.

The Jäger Bombs arrived and this time Marie-Anne took it upon herself to make a toast, 'After these shots, I'd like to hear the uncensored version of how this song came about and what it means to X.'

Bell and Anton cheered to this. Xolani smiled and tipped his head in her direction before they all took their shots simultaneously.

'Speech!' Bell howled into his ear. He tried to sway out of her way but she continued leaning into him.

'This is how I get bullied!' he told Anton and Marie-Anne, who giggled at the display. When Bell allowed him to sit upright again, he ran his hands through his dreads and looked up to an expectant audience.

'Wow, um ... okay, how do we start this story? There was so much that happened that led to us getting to the place. We kind of fell on it, right?' he said to

Anton, who took his cue to chip in.

'Ja. But the easiest place to start would be the fact that our managers wanted our two bands to meet and see if we could do a collaboration. Which, to be honest, X, I'd been wanting to do for a very long time. I just loved your guys' sound, even if I couldn't understand most of what you were saying,' Anton admitted.

'I know this is going to sound corny, but I was thinking the same. This might sound lame, but I kind of looked at you guys and your fans as, like, the Afrikaans versions of us.' Everyone laughed. 'But really, I just felt we were probably discussing the same things with different audiences,' Xolani added.

'I can see that,' Bell nodded, biting her lip. Marie-Anne also nodded her agreement.

'Ja, anyway, our managers set up a dinner, like down the road here, at Papa's. And it was a little bit stiff at first,' Anton chortled.

Xolani continued, 'Yeah, it was kind of this meeting of two worlds. Our band on one side of the table and you guys on the other side. And we were wondering, like, what kind of white boys you guys were.'

The table shared a giggle.

'On our side we were thinking, like, how are these black ous going to treat us?' Anton chimed.

'Anyway, long story short, enough food and liquor later, we were the last patrons at the restaurant. I think one of our managers knew the owner or something.'

'Ja, it's Stefan's brother,' said Anton.

'Told you one of them did. So anyway, it turned out that these guys are the kind of white boys we could get down with. We're eventually forced out of the restaurant at, like, three in the morning. But not before we got a bottle of whiskey and brandewyn. Then, Marius, also known as Hond, decides that we have to go to Nelspruit!' he added.

'Fokken hell!' Marie-Anne exclaimed.

'Hey, you said you wanted to hear the uncensored version.' Xolani lifted his shoulders and his hands, palms turned upward. 'So, for some reason, we thought "Nelspruit" was some Pretoria club where Afrikaans kids get down.'

They all laughed.

He continued, 'Anyway, Stefan's brother let us borrow one of his shuttles that he usually uses to pick up and drop off his employees, we pile in and Hond decides that he's gonna drive. Firstly, I don't know why Stefan's brother thought this was in any way a good idea. Secondly, it was decided that Jerry had to ride up front and keep Hond awake – honestly, I don't know what we were thinking. These drunk guys falling over each other and deciding to drive to Nelspruit. Mind you, Jerry, Ndumo and me still think that this is some elaborate joke and that we're just going to a place in Pretoria North or some shit, so I figure cool, here's my wallet for the toll gates as my contribution and decide to catch a kip. Little did we know that we're actually about to drive 146 kilometres *outside* of Nelspruit! Ndumo's in the seat behind me next to Ruan. Jerry is obviously riding shotgun, Anton's stretched out in the back and sleeping on Ruan's lap. I don't know how Hond and Jerry pulled it off. I have my suspicions.' He smiled and cocked his brow before rubbing his nose with his index finger and thumb a few times and sniffing. He continued before anyone got a chance to respond, 'But five hours later, we're still passed out and being woken up by Jerry and Hond screaming, "We're at the fucking Potholes!"'

'Wait, where was JT in all of this?' Bell interrupted.

'That dude's got kids, so he doesn't come to meetings he doesn't think are necessary. You know how he is. Anyway, we're still trying to bring the world into focus, still pissed and all shocked cause we didn't know where the fuck we were. Jerry and Hond are laughing at us, saying that this is exactly where we said we were headed.'

'Nee!' Marie-Anne exclaimed, clasping her hand to her mouth.

'This is easily the most ridiculous and retarded story I've ever heard!' Bell said to the table. Marie-Anne agreed enthusiastically with her sentiments. Their waiter returned; they ordered another round of cocktails and Marie-Anne added another round of shots.

'Marie-Anne!' Anton exclaimed in mock surprise.

'Ag, ja, I think we might as well sommer make our way to Mapumalanga tonight!' she joked. 'Okay, and then?' she pressed Xolani, who was forced to gulp the cocktail he had intended to sip.

'Oh yeah, so it turns out Jerry had some shrooms with him from Grietfest, where we all played but didn't actually meet,' he replied.

'Ja, that crowd was fucking mental!' Anton added.

'He'd actually forgotten that he had them and sort of just found them in his pockets when we got there. And actually, no one else wanted to take, so it was only me and Anton who chowed the shrooms for breakfast. Now, can you imagine the sight of these lumbering Afrikaans hulks, two of them with long-ass hair, rolling around with three skinny black guys, all taking swigs from the bottles we had? Luckily, we were, like, the first people there and so we could lie down on the bridges unencumbered. God, it was fucking amazing!'

'Ja, the waterfalls crashing all around you to the point that you could feel the bridge vibrate. I think we all lay down on the bridge for a little bit, but the other okes didn't really feel the same thing we were feeling. I don't know, at least for me; the sun on my skin, the roar of the waterfalls with that tiny little spray of water reaching easily and the shaking of the bridge was so fucking ...' Anton trailed off with a glint of nostalgia in his eye, his baby teeth almost showing. 'Ja,' he said, more to himself than anyone else, and looked down at his hands on the table. A Jäger Bomb and fresh cocktail were suddenly placed in the spot he had been staring at longingly. Marie-Anne rubbed his arm before they all took their shots.

Then she pressed Xolani again about the song.

'So yeah, it was a pretty wild experience, being in the presence of such great natural features, you know? Like, of course the shrooms helped with, like, the sensory experience or whatever, but I guess I had this really crazy existential moment, you know? Like remembering just how small we all are in the greater scheme of things. I had this, like, sudden, I don't know how to describe it … but it was this weird, almost painful tickle in my core. And listening to the crash of the waterfalls, I guess I felt the rumble of a song I hadn't heard sung in, like, forever.' He paused to take a sip of his drink. Bell put her fingers in his hair and began to massage his head. He stared out onto Burnett Street's increasing foot traffic coming to life in the night.

'It was a song my uncle sang to me at initiation school. The song itself speaks about the burden of remaining in perpetual childhood and calls on men to attest to that fact. It then calls on the spirit of the great warrior who initiated the custom to affirm that the statement is in fact true.' He smiled at his companions, who seemed to be looking at him with a vague admiration.

They began to talk about how wonderful the

sentiment was and how brave he was to go through that. That although the practice sounded barbaric, it also sounded like it could be beautiful. A heaviness had started to weigh on him as the memories of his time spent on that mountain revealed themselves to him at the table. He had learnt truths that he had been denying since his time there. He smiled and nodded as if listening to the conversation, but couldn't help himself from being dragged back to the day he first heard the song.

\*

'Ufana no nyoko kwedini!' Uncle Zweli accused his nephew. 'Actually, you know, I think it's great that you took after her in the way that you look,' he said staring at his nephew, who had the same annoying habit of a constantly shifting gaze that his late older brother had had. 'I never trusted her you know ... your mother. Anyone that your father was able to fool, I find suspicious.' He paused. 'But to be fair to her, she had never known me, so I shouldn't fault her too harshly.' Uncle Zweli lazily shifted his weight, awkwardly calling attention to his locked knee by moaning about the pain every time he moved it. His crying about it and refusal to have it properly looked at was an annoyance to his nephew.

The constant expression of these mild aches served to conceal a hurt that he had never expressed to Xolani. He had been hard on this boy, who should have been his son. The reason he had accepted his mother's invitation to live with them for two years was so he could teach him exactly who he was. This boy who, instead of having searched for and taken pride in his identity, had instead embraced the very world he had been fighting against. And the boy's mother, who in another life could have been his wife, had instead taken the very white man he had fought, as a husband.

He watched Xolani with a contemptuous scowl before gruffly speaking again, 'Do you not get tired of wondering what people are saying all the time? Not fully understanding any language you speak? To not be able to laugh at a joke with complete certainty that you understood its full meaning, rather than observing social protocols? To not always wonder whether you're the butt of it or not? I really don't understand; you seem to take pride in your ignorance instead of being ashamed enough to ask more questions to learn about yourselves.'

The words stung Xolani and made him feel smaller than he had in all the time he'd been there. The isolation was already something that had almost enveloped him upon his arrival, but he took on the solitude, stone faced, in the hope that his uncle would recognise him as his own. But instead he was suffering another rejection from the only person whose approval he sought. His uncle had a habit of shunning him without regard for his feelings, with the assumption that everything he said to his nephew didn't land anyway. He was unaware of the role that he had played in Xolani's career pursuits; he looked down on his music career as fleeting and meaningless without giving it a single listen. The fact that the songs were on radio did not move him in the slightest. His uncle barely recalled the afternoons they spent together on the grass singing, and that had been the catalyst for Xolani's pursuit of music. His nephew couldn't find a way to tell him how he had learnt to express himself in those times and how it was those memories that had birthed his love for singing.

They sat on a rock as dusk approached, looking out at a stream in front of them. The katabatic winds carried a chill with them as they made their way down the mountain slopes, greeting the paternal pair as they passed. Surrounded by shrubs and rich greenery, they heard the makeshift community of Xolani's initiate peers behind them in conversations punctuated with laughter. The ashes of the clay Xolani was expected to cake himself with daily caught a ride on the passing breeze. More of his brown skin peeped through his masked face.

'You know that your father and I never got along?' Uncle Zweli asked him.

Xolani nodded without looking at his uncle.

'You also know that he was a policeman?'

Xolani nodded again, looking out at the tops of the trees that the view allowed them.

'I told your mother I was going to tell you the truth about your father up here; there's no better place to be pained and heal.'

Xolani looked at his uncle for the first time since his visit that day with confusion knotting his face.

'Let me tell you about where that inheritance money that you're playing around with comes from. I fought for the country, while your father served those who stole it from us and helped them beat and keep us in chains.' His uncle started talking while rolling a joint using newspaper.

Xolani knew that his uncle expected him to smoke with him. Since his arrival, he had always been expected to smoke when offered. He had never enjoyed the sensation of getting high on weed but could not afford to decline niceties in a ritual custom that he was foreign to, yet a part of.

'We hadn't spoken in twenty years, me and my brother. We were different people. He was always a neat freak and a stickler for rules, while I was his unkempt, quiet, younger brother. Like you, we looked like our mother and I was just as quiet as she was growing up. My brother was the apple of my father's eye. Even after—' Uncle Zweli put the rolled newspaper into his mouth, struck a match, cupped it in his hands and bowed his head to light it. Smoke fell through his hands as he exhaled. He raised his head and looked to the skies, taking another drag. He blew out a loud cloud that wisped away to meet its heavenly cousins above them. Xolani watched his profile turn into silhouette.

'*Especially* after he became a policeman for the boers,' he continued, without acknowledging his pause.

He passed his crude joint to Xolani, ignoring his reluctance. 'See, my brother's biggest problem was the fact that I took his place as the family favourite when I left home to fight his masters. Not because my parents were political. If anything, they were apathetic to the cause. I only became their favourite because they never knew what became of me. I learnt that they had both died heartbroken, forcing my brother to promise them that he'd find me and bring me back home safe.'

After pulling a few times from the end of the newspaper's wet fish tail, Xolani gave it back to his uncle. He remained quiet. When Uncle Zweli took the joint from him, they locked eyes for a moment.

'See, I didn't think your father was a sellout for being a cop. I mean, the job isn't much different to being a nurse, postman or bus driver, to be honest. No, I hated your father for the person he was.'

Without warning Uncle Zweli burst into a long

soulful cry that bounced off the rocks of the mountains and was swallowed by the vegetation, 'Ubukwekwe inetyala! Vumani madoda!'

Silence fell in the aftermath of the wail. Even the other initiates were stilled by the call. He gave the joint back to Xolani and cupped his hands around his mouth to add more verve to the melancholic call. 'Ubukwekwe inetyala! Vumani madoda!'

This time a chorus of deep voices from Xolani's peers responded, 'Siyavuma!'

Xolani felt further antagonised by his uncle's flippant display of communal expression and belonging.

'Did you ever ask your mother how she met your father? I guess she would have never told you the truth anyway. Once our parents died, your daddy did go out looking for me. But not out of love. He did it seeking vengeance for my having usurped our parents' affection from him. His fragile sense of self couldn't bear the demotion and so he hunted me. But instead of doing it like any other man would, he did it through the services of his masters. The man who made you,' he spat at the ground, 'rather than seeking out his last surviving family member – who was fighting for his very freedom even if he didn't deserve it – out of an elder brother's love, he sought an impotent revenge.'

Xolani was beginning to feel overwhelmed by the information being rattled off at him by the uncle whom he'd secretly called father. It was as if a double betrayal was being committed against him. His breath became shorter and he felt as if the world was slipping further away from him. For the first time, he was reaching the realisation of how alien his surroundings were, how unfamiliar he was with the tongues spoken around and to him. And more, he was conscious of his distance from the person he'd always looked to for paternal guidance. He felt hot and cold at the truth of his conception and a slight vexation towards his mother for having betrayed him; to have this story told to him by his uncle's bitter tongue.

Again, without warning, Uncle Zweli called out to the dying light being consumed by a navy blanket and replaced with shy twinkles. 'Ubukwekwe inetyala! Vumani madoda!'

'Siyavuma!' they called back.

'Vumani madoda!'

'Siyavuma!'

'Vumani madoda!'

'Siyavuma!'

The melancholy of his uncle's call and the simplicity of the words hurt something deep inside Xolani. Uncle Zweli was driving the point home that a flesh wound was the least severe part of being birthed into adulthood.

As was his wont, Uncle Zweli returned to his story without acknowledgement of the pause. 'Our camp in Lusaka was raided and we were taken unawares. My escape and subsequent return are stories far too long to tell. But I was missing in action for quite some time.'

Uncle Zweli had never spoken about his time in exile in any meaningful way. There were small mutterings whenever he'd finished smoking his beloved weed, or passing anecdotes, but never anything of substance. Once they were old enough, Nthabiseng and Xolani realised that his inability to sleep was probably a direct result of the time he had spent fighting. But this was the first time he was talking explicitly to Xolani about it.

He spat at the ground another time before he continued, 'My time away was enough to allow the boers to collect intel at our camp and to plant my brother as a spy inside the security apparatus. When enough time had passed, they sent him to Johannesburg with a story about escaping torture, made plausible by the intelligence they had on me and what they were able to gather at the camp. Me and your father always looked alike. I guess I don't have to tell you that – the first time you met me you thought that I was him.' He left his words hanging in the air before he continued, 'Our likeness even got us in trouble when we were young. It's funny cause no one else in our family saw that. Your snake of a father was able to infiltrate a group in Johannesburg by passing himself off as me. Of course there were suspicions, especially when people saw me suddenly appear out of nowhere after the raid. But he and his boers were able to come up with a story that fooled the ones in charge there. In his double life as me, he found your mother, who was a student at the time.'

Xolani felt as if he was sinking into the ground learning the true nature of the father who his mother had always described as a strong character, which to him translated to being principled. He studied the contempt on Uncle Zweli's face, desperately searching for the love he once looked at him with.

'I always thought that I'd find it in me to love you as my own regardless of your father's deeds. After all, he impregnated your mother pretending to be his little faggot brother ... but the truth is, I've never found anything in you to make me proud,' Uncle Zweli declared.

Xolani felt as if he was in free fall and Uncle Zweli's words echoed around him in the darkness. As he watched his uncle's outline fade, he fell further.

'You've never had to fight for anything and no rite of passage will make you a man. I come from a place where my childhood ended when I had to fight for our country's future and yet you're all I have to show for it. I have to admit to myself, at this point, that all I did was fight for you and that little coloured sister of yours to be the exact kind of blacks that the whites want you to be. The same as your mother. It makes sense that she found my brother. But a man never escapes divine justice. It's true your father died in a car accident.

It's just ironic, that it happened on his way to beg for amnesty from the commission,' Uncle Zweli said, fixing a malevolent smile on his face.

He looked his nephew in the eye for an extended moment, before rising off the rock and shooting off the final barb of the exchange,

'Ubukwekwe inetyala! Vumani madoda!'
'Siyavuma!'
'Vumani madoda!'
'Siyavuma!'
'Vumani madoda!'
'Ubukwekwe inetyala! Vumani madoda!'
'Siyavuma!'
'Vumani madoda!'
'Siyavuma!'
'Somagwaza kawuvume!'
'Somagwaza kawuvume bo!'
'Siyavuma!'

The wind's chill that night on the mountain could not have been colder.

\*

He was brought back to the present by Bell using his shoulder to lift herself from her seat in making her way to the bathroom.

'He has a habit of losing himself inside his head

at random times,' she said to Anton and Marie-Anne, who were looking at him with curious smiles.

Xolani pulled himself out of the past and drunkenly slurred that it was time for more shots, to which there was unanimous agreement.

*

Staying up to watch the sunrise, while the others slept, left her time to stumble over her own thoughts. Staring at the dawn about to break over the city gave her the brief solitude she had hoped for the previous night. She took in the different colours of the city lights illuminating the dark patches interspersed on the horizon. She felt the dryness at the back of her throat and tasted a sweetened staleness in her mouth. She reached for the vodka and Coke in front of her and curled her lips as the pungent syrup hit her palate. She noticed that Joan had left her cigarettes on the table and helped herself. She lit the tip and, as she inhaled, she carefully listened for the crisp burning of the tobacco and paper, while its amber eye glowered at her. Whenever she inhaled, she allowed the smoke to first hit the back of her throat and let it swirl around her mouth before gently exhaling, allowing a thick plume to cascade out of her mouth.

'I got to admit, that looks pretty fucking nice,' she

said aloud to herself. She watched the tendrils of smoke float away into the sky and redirected her focus to the city lights fighting for relevance against the impending daylight. She looked out into the wide network of mostly empty roads, streets, avenues and lanes. Every now and again, she observed moving white lights pass red ones. They appeared and vanished intermittently. She took in the reds, greens and ambers performing their tasks regardless of the day's mood, whilst listening to increasing chirps and the distant groans and rumbles of motors. Watching the day's traffic gradually begin, she noticed that cars, like people, were in a constant state of passing each other with little to no acknowledgement of the other. No hoots or flickers of cognisance that would indicate the individual lives they were all living. It was all a web of blank recognition. Sticking to their lanes yet noting the presence of the other; 'Just don't get too close, or we'll hurt each other'.

She imagined the kinds of conversations taking place in the cars. She could see tiny versions of herself and her brother driving away from visiting their mother's home, as they listened to her describe the ways in which change would help her family. The pair were highly attentive, hoping to understand most of what their mother was saying. They were outcasts on these family visits, treated differently to all the other children. They had always chosen to stick together and out of shyness didn't try pronouncing the words of the language the other children spoke, for fear of being laughed at. While they could for the most part make out what was being said, the children of the township spoke to them in their own broken version of the language that the two had grown up with. Neither Nthabiseng nor Xolani could make out whether this was their way of marking them as different or an attempt to accommodate them. It was hard for them to figure out the motives of the other children. Some openly mocked them, both in their own language and what they assumed were impressions of them speaking in high-pitched nasal voices and rounded vowels that mimicked grotesque American accents. They simply smiled, nodded, shook their heads and made the constant choice to rather observe the play of the other children than participate in their games.

    They had watched their mother, Masechaba, trying to be as helpful as possible around the house but could always see the way people rolled their eyes behind her back, pulled faces and seemed not to take anything she said seriously. Yet she was the person they depended on to provide them with groceries, help their kids through school and take care of their living conditions. There was a silent resentment to her presence, along with an expectation of charity to meet all wants, needs and desires that could not be obtained through their own hands. It seemed that whenever she arrived, hunger grew tenfold, and people had unexpected preferences for goods they could not usually afford. Suddenly, the need for milk was equated to that of cold drink, which turned into a beer, beer into brandy and brandy, whiskey.

A younger Masechaba had swept through the house in the early years with a modernity that was at first resisted. But her enthusiasm to replace the old with the new, and the dusty for the shiny, created new spaces within the home. Where there once stood a room divider – a massive cupboard that housed the TV, VCR and cassette deck, framed by shelved crockery housed in glass doors; a built-in cabinet stuffed with miscellaneous official documents: from bills to receipts to warranties, as well as framed pictures of different members of the family – now stood a simple TV stand with a satellite decoder and the latest PlayStation. The disappearance of the room divider exposed the dinner table, once hidden from view. It had stood between the passage to the bathroom and the children's bedroom. It was also conveniently placed adjacent to the kitchen where Masechaba spent most of her time as a child with her sisters and cousins. Nthabiseng recalled her mother explaining that it was where they were expected to cook and wait on being summoned to serve their parents' guests, as and when needed.

Musing over the room divider, Masechaba described not being able to occupy communal space with adults in the evenings when their guests would regularly arrive. If they were not making themselves useful in the kitchen, they were expected to be in their bedroom, out of sight. Walking from the kitchen to the bedroom or bathroom, they were shielded from the vista of adults in conversation by the imposing piece of furniture. Masechaba speculated that the room divider was an enforcement that the house was not an open space where people of all ages fraternised, and the hierarchy was fixed through it. You could hear elders, but were not to speak to them. The elders rarely wanted to hear from the children, save to indulge the frivolities of youth, after which they were to retreat into a quiet solitude of immaturity, blocking out the normative daily humiliation of arbitrary discrimination enforced by the rule of law.

In the car rides to and from this house, Nthabiseng and Xolani listened to Masechaba speaking about her experiences at home and her criticisms of some of the ways in which she was brought up to believe that everything had a box in which it had to remain. She said that her family couldn't recognise how much space the home contained until the clutter was removed. She called the room divider an unnatural way to separate the flow of the house: it suited the appetites of the infrastructure that forced them to animate the tiny boxes they were assigned for not being born on the right side of apartheid. And how easily they had accepted that position. She spoke about the change of environment once they opened up the space. A simple TV stand gave everyone a view of the whole house and a means to communicate openly with one another, rather than closing themselves off to the rigid social hierarchies that they brought from the outside into their homes. Being diminutised to boys and girls forced her parents to further infantilise (their) children as a tool to retain a power they couldn't wield anywhere else. This assumed lore of African elder superiority meant that they cut themselves off from the advances of the world. New ideas became taboos that were against custom. Custom, she said, had itself been forced into shape by the laws of the day. It was used as an excuse to keep static what should be dynamic. Rather than allowing new ways of being to evolve, Masechaba's parents and their generation would reinforce customs designed to maintain power for those with little imagination and who were wholly unappreciative of movement.

'You guys must remember that those without power always covet it for their own gain. If only they could understand that shared perspectives and triumphs forward depend on multiple and divergent opinions,' she'd say.

'Mama,' Xolani would suddenly interject, 'what does "covet" mean?'

It would be at this stage that Masecaba would look

at her frowning children and realise that she had lost them and had been talking mostly to herself. She'd forget at times that they were children and that they weren't ready to take on the burdens of liberal thinking to shape the world that they were to occupy. To their credit, they always seemed fascinated by her thoughts and didn't often interrupt her. And that's why she often found herself rambling away with little to no word from them. It could not be said that they were disinterested. Rather, they were yet to develop so that they could be active participants in the conversation, instead of vacant sponges, who merely caught strings of thought with arms too weak to hold the weight of her arguments.

'You guys must stop Mama when she's doing all the talking!' she told them.

'No Mama, we're listening!' the precocious pair would egg her on.

'That's enough of Mummy's nonsense,' she would say, driving them back from their last visit to their grandparents' home. 'Xoli, don't you want to play the KTV CD so we can all sing and make this a fun car?!'

Always his mother's co-pilot, Xolani obliged. And from start to end, the rest of trip would be a howling of bad cover songs sung by child presenters from the popular Kids TV show.

These trips became less frequent as Nthabiseng and Xolani grew older and more alert to the short, shared thoughts of their mother's relatives. They increasingly felt less and less welcomed by her family. After the passing on of their grandmother, there was no one to protect them from the cold shoulders of resentful cousins, now unwilling to take their mute English-speaking cousins around the neighbourhood for fear of embarrassment.

\*

Nthabiseng shifted in her seat and put an elbow on the table. In doing so she knocked over her glass and spilt its contents. The moment's clumsiness brought her back to the current day as she quickly needed to calculate which items to save from drowning. She managed to save only the cigarettes. The three phones on the table were left to bathe in the liquor and she made no attempt to grab them or to clean the table. After a final drag of the cigarette, she flicked it off the balcony and made a languorous effort to get to the kitchen and find a substitute for the spilt drink. Plopping herself back into her seat, she helped herself to another one of Joan's cigarettes and went back to watching the city sprawled out in front of her. A wave of guilt washed over her as she remembered that she hadn't replied to her mother's message. Thinking better of returning the call right there and then, she made a mental note to get back to her later that morning. Spotting at her feet the cider that she had fetched from the fridge, she picked it up and made a feeble attempt to twist off its cap. She failed at her first attempt and her second attempt was even more pathetic. She panted aloud, exaggerating her efforts.

'Jesus!' Monique commented from the door. 'Just open the fucking thing already!'

On her third attempt, the cap came off. She lifted the bottle.

'Victory at last!' she slurred smugly at her friend.

Spotting the mess that Nthabiseng had made, Monique rushed over to the table and picked up the phones left pickling in the sticky pool.

'Seriously, what the fuck?!' she asked, turning with the phones in her hand.

'Oh yeah,' Nthabiseng said with a smirk. 'That happened; meant to call someone about it.'

Monique gave her a sharp stare and reprimanded her, 'You're fucked. Go sleep, drink coffee or whatever, but this is not fucking cool!'

'I'm sorry,' she said casting down her eyes. Then she pepped up instantly, 'So there's still some shit in the fridge. What say you get yourself a drink and we watch the silent city come to life and light with the peeping sun?' she asked with as sweet a smile as she could muster.

Monique glared at her for a moment, before leaving and returning with a bottle of her own, taking a seat next to Nthabiseng.

'So, you've just left your squeeze?' Nthabiseng asked.

Monique didn't respond. Instead, she took her turn to stare out at the city. Nthabiseng took this as a cue to do the same. Her thoughts were about her friend sitting next to her. The friend she'd grown up with since they met at pre-school, aged four. Monique's hair was the deep, dark brown that could almost be mistaken for black. She always looked like she was pouting and it didn't help that she was a serial snacker, which meant that her mouth constantly attracted attention. They'd been in the same sport teams since they started Grade 1 together and, barring a year or two, somehow always found themselves in the same classes. Often, they took each other for granted, knowing that no matter how much they fought, their making up was inevitable.

Monique was one of those bilingual kids who fought very hard to keep her Afrikaner origins as private as possible. She was an only child with a frigid mother and a father who fawned over her. Nthabiseng remembered how she was once forced to eat onions at the breakfast table by Monique's mother, Jana. Jana had scolded her, saying that she didn't believe in waste and expected all children at her table to be grateful for the food they were given. Nthabiseng tried to explain that she was allergic to onions; when questioned about her allergy, she explained that onions made her puke. Jana dismissed this as 'fussiness'.

'Nthabi, in hierdie huis eet ons ons kos klaar. Ek weet nie wat by jou pa se huis gebeur nie, maar dis wat hier gebeur. Maak asseblief jou kos klaar,' Jana instructed. She always insisted on speaking Afrikaans to Nthabiseng, telling her that she should never forget or be ashamed of her father's language. A terse and strict disciplinarian, Jana rarely let the girls get away with anything under her watch and never missed an opportunity to let them know how spoilt they were. As a result, over the years, Monique became a third sibling in Nthabiseng's home as the distance between her and her mother grew. Jana, in turn, became resentful of the mongrel child and family that she felt had stolen her daughter from her own family.

The entire incident mortified Monique. When they had finished eating, Nthabiseng ran to the bathroom, feeling the sick on its way up. They were only eight back then, but Monique picked a fight with her mother about embarrassing her in front of her best friend. Nthabiseng listened to the entire ordeal from upstairs and heard Monique's wailing as her mother spanked her for being disrespectful. Monique ran upstairs to join Nthabiseng in her room, eyes swollen, and called her father to come and take them to his house. Her father made up for his absence after the divorce by listening to every demand his daughter made, regardless of its irrationality.

Staring out from the balcony, Nthabiseng couldn't help but be affected by all the love she felt for her friend. They didn't often share such sentiments with each other, mainly because Monique wasn't the kind to show overt affection, but there was a tacit understanding of how much they meant to each other.

Nthabiseng broke the silence, 'Can you believe in a couple of short months it'll all be done and we'll be doing things like this at will? The big bad world awaits us and here we sit with no plans on how we're going to handle it.'

Monique remained silent, still staring at the city and taking a sip of her drink from time to time. Nthabiseng lit another cigarette.

She turned to Monique and said, 'Fuck, I'm sorry about the phones! Jesus!'

'Was that so hard?' Monique said, finally looking at her.

'It was,' said Nthabiseng. 'Now quit your bitchy ways and tell me why you're out of bed so early and not spooning with Jason.'

Monique looked back out at the city and took a sip of her drink.

'I feel like Wimpy,' Nthabiseng suddenly said as the thought struck her.

'That's the first time you've made any sense since I stepped out onto this balcony,' Monique replied.

*

Saturday sun rushed through Thami's bedroom windows and landed on his face. He opened and shut his eyes, giving them a chance to adjust to the daylight. He kicked off the duvet and stretched his entire body to reach for all the corners of the bed. Lifting his back off the mattress, he indulged in a large open-mouthed yawn. He swung his legs off the bed, rested his elbows on his knees and took in the patterns of the carpet that his feet rested on. He reached for the phone on his bedside table; she still hadn't responded to his text. He felt resentful and embarrassed at the same time. He silently lamented sending the message in the first place and wished that the app had a delete function. He let his toes feel the nubs of the carpet for a while. Then he stood up and stretched a second time, reaching for the ceiling on the tips of his toes.

He slid his feet into his slippers, pulled on the T-shirt he had worn the day before from the floor, opened the door and descended the staircase just outside his room. As he rounded the corner of the passage that led to the kitchen, he heard an engine start in the garage. The gentle pull-off confirmed that it was his mother. This meant he had been spared the complaints that were sure to come, for walking around the house in his boxers.

He opened the fridge and stared at its contents for a while, trying to decide what he wanted to have for breakfast. His mind was still a bit foggy and it took a second or two to properly register the contents on the cooled shelves. Although breakfast was the hardest meal for him to eat, because he was hardly ever hungry in the mornings, he knew that he needed it for the energy. He scanned the shelves with a listless boredom, his eyes finally landing on a tub of plain white Bulgarian yoghurt that he decided he'd have with a bowl of muesli. After finding the muesli, he grabbed a bowl and spoon and set to mixing the ingredients on the kitchen table. After putting everything back in its place, he made his way to the TV room.

He flipped through channels looking for something worthwhile. He landed on the news and saw that student protests had been going on since Friday at the TUT campus. He finished his food and got up to leave the room, switching off the TV. At the entrance of the room he met his father who had a newspaper in his hand. They smiled at each other and his father looked at his legs and raised his eyebrows when they re-established eye contact.

Thami nodded, raised his bowl and motioned that

he was on his way to the kitchen. His father stepped out of the way, allowing him to pass. Thami washed his bowl and spoon in the kitchen scullery, dried them off, put them back in their places and headed for his room. As he reached the staircase his mother emerged from the garage sooner than he had expected. She wore a long tan dress that almost touched her ankles, with gold hoop earrings and her hair in a neat ponytail resting on the front of her left shoulder. Her dress matched her skin tone and he almost asked if she was trying out the new camouflage trend. She had grocery bags in both hands and stopped at the sight of him.

'Morning, Ma.'

'Papa ...' she started, without returning his greeting, 'how many times have I told you that it is just not decent to walk around the house in your panties?'

He couldn't suppress his smile, 'Askies, Mme. I was on my way to go shower.'

'Mara Thami, di tsebe tsa hao, do they even work? It's like something goes in one side and immediately flies out the other. I bet that you went to eat and watch TV before this sudden idea to go wash! Mara Thami! Sometimes a ke itsi gore ke etseng. You just don't listen to me! Go wash yourself before I lose my temper!'

As he ascended the stairs she continued, her voice rising with every word.

'You come and sit among people when you haven't even washed your face and brushed your teeth and then still have the cheek to do it all in your panties! Is that normal? What kind of child are you? Just have some respect, damn it!' she shouted until he finally closed the bathroom door.

After getting dressed, he decided it wasn't the kind of day he wanted to spend at home and thought he might be able to get some kicks by checking out the TUT campus. Maybe there'd be some damage he could snap. He walked into the lounge where his father sat reading the paper, facing the switched-off TV. Thami stood at his shoulder and told him that he was going for a drive and wasn't sure when he'd be back. His father didn't put down his paper or make any sound to acknowledge the information. But Thami knew that he had been heard.

With his camera in hand, he opened his car door and dropped it on the passenger seat. He pressed the button for the garage door to open, reversed into the driveway and closed the door properly before prepping to pull out into the street. As he started to reverse again, he spotted a car at the entrance of his driveway, which turned, drove in and came to a halt right next to his. The sudden appearance of the car took him by complete surprise. He got out of his own and studied the Polo in his parents' driveway. He recognised the metallic blue but was trying to figure out where from.

He walked around the car and peered through the windshield before making his way to the driver's door.

He recognised the bald guy in the passenger seat as the rugby captain at his school, and the driver as one of Nthabiseng's friends. As he leaned towards the window to speak to them, he realised that they looked as confused as he was.

'Hi?' he said to them. They both burst into laughter. Thami frowned at them, still confused by their presence.

'So ... Um ... Hi?' the driver said to him in a fit of giggles.

Thami's expression changed from confused to annoyed.

'So, what are you doing at my house?' he asked.

The rugby player pulled down his shades with a finger to sit on the edge of his nose, revealing his bloodshot eyes. He then motioned to the backseat with his thumb. Thami's eyes followed the direction the thumb had sent them to, and he saw her in the back seat, passed out with her dreads resting on the window. He stared at her and then back at Tumi, the driver, who was trying to suppress her giggling. She told him that she had just put the address into the GPS and followed its directions. Apparently, Nthabiseng had promised her friends an adventure. She then turned around and shook Nthabiseng's leg, waking her with a start. Nthabiseng stared at the car's occupants with a shocked expression, and then out of the open window. She looked at Thami and started smiling. She rubbed the corners of her mouth with the back of her hand, in case any spittle had taken up residence there.

'Well, this is not embarrassing,' she said in a husky whisper. Her eyes were glossy and bright red, with webs on her corneas suggesting little sleep. She fumbled with the door handle and almost fell out of the car. She stood in the driveway, stretched and yawned while looking at him. 'We're going for breakfast, there's space in the car.' She looked at him with her eyes almost closed.

'This car is way over the limit. They wouldn't even need a breathalyser for this one,' Thami told her.

'Hey!' Tumi called for his attention, 'Did I hit you, your car or your garage?'

'That's a bar I'd trip over, it's so low,' he thought but didn't voice. He looked at Tumi and smiled. 'You didn't hit anything, no,' he replied.

'So ... are you in or out?' Nthabiseng asked.

'As flattering as this invitation is, I think I'm going to have to go with "out",' he shrugged.

'Well, we tried. Come Nthabiseng, let's go,' Tumi said, unmoved by the response.

Nthabiseng hadn't taken her eyes off Thami. 'It looks like you were on your way out,' she said to him. 'I'll just jump in with you.' She closed the Polo's door and went straight to Thami's car, opened the passenger door and picked up his camera from the seat.

'Hey, this might come in handy,' she said dangling

the camera by its strap. She sat herself down and closed the door.

'Cool,' Tumi said. 'Guess you guys are going to follow us,' she announced to him and reversed out of the driveway. She turned out into the street, idling while waiting for Thami to start his car. The front door of the house opened; Thami's father stood there and looked at him. Thami looked back at him, got in his car and realised that Nthabiseng had passed out against his car's window this time. Without sparing his father another glance, he pulled out of the driveway and followed the Polo.

Driving out of the suburb, he saw that the Polo was headed for the main road, which he thought was a bad idea considering the driver's state. He watched as the car speeding along in front of him flirted with the solid line of the road and was convinced that if there was a roadblock they'd definitely be pulled over. As the thought crossed his mind, there they were. Right by the Waterglen Shopping Centre on Garsfontein Road stood the cops. Their usual haunt. The Polo slowed down and tried to drive in a straight line as they approached the robots, just ahead of the waiting roadblock. The robot changed from red to green and they were off; Thami followed the Polo into the belly of the beast.

'Nthabiseng,' he called. But it was no use. Her dreads were plastered to the window. He watched the police signal for the Polo to carry on and waited for the same as he inched behind them. No such luck. The head against the window seemed to have attracted the attention of a cop ready to extort some money out of a member of the young *nouveau riche*. Thami slowed the car down and pulled over to the side of the road.

Once the car was at a complete standstill, one of the cops sauntered over. Cap atop his head, boots carrying a heavyset body, he took his time walking to them. Thami slid down his window as he got closer. The man eventually stood in front of Thami's window, wearing a kevlar vest with the word 'POLICE' printed on it. He stretched next to the window, bending his back, giving Thami a better view of the gun in his holster. The man then took off his cap, leaned in through the window and Thami saw his bald head beaded with sweat. Before saying anything, the officer took out a handkerchief and used one of Thami's mirrors to look at his reflection as he wiped the sweat off his head. Thami sat in an awkward silence as he watched the display. When it looked like it was over, Thami decided to initiate conversation.

'O kae, ntate?' He immediately regretted his choice of words. He had greeted the policeman in the singular instead of the more polite and less direct plural; in this way, he had made this matter about the two of them alone.

'Iyoh, moshimane, it's hot, hey?' the man said. 'Eish, mara you're in a Ford Fiesta with an air conditioner, so I'm sure you don't know what I'm talking about.'

Thami laughed at the joke.

The man looked at him, feigning shock, 'Or is that a lie that I'm telling?'

'Eish, ntate, it's only nice for people to fall asleep in, really,' he deflected and tried to steer the friendly conversation away from where it would inevitably end.

'Really?' he asked with his enthusiastic demeanour.

'It's true,' Thami replied with a quiet smile.

'So then, tell me, where are you guys coming from?'

'I was here at home, ntate.' The situation did not fit the statement and he knew it.

'So, tell me, where are you headed to now?' the policeman enquired.

'We're on our way to eat breakfast,' Thami replied.

'So, how's she now going to eat breakfast in her sleep?' he asked in mock confusion.

'I'll just have to wake her up, ntate.'

'Wow! It must be great to live in the suburb of Garsfontein. So, tell me then, what were you guys doing last night?' the cop pressed on.

'Well, I don't know what she was up to; she came to me like this.' He was really trying to figure out how to best answer the questions asked of him, but each answer sounded more ridiculous than the last.

'So, vele, what do you know? And wena? Why are you awake when your person here is fast asleep, but you still want breakfast? What kind of Viagra are you using?'

Thami laughed, unable to control himself. 'It's not like that, ntate,' was all he could say, as he tried to compose himself again.

'So, this girlfriend of yours ... what is she? Is she a coloured?'

Thami was stunned by the question and recoiled at the policeman's descriptor. He didn't know how to answer. To make things a little easier for himself, he affirmed the policeman's guess. The policeman, who had been happy leaning on the car, suddenly stuck his head in past Thami to get a better look at the passed-out passenger. He sniffed at her, then drew his head back out the window and informed Thami that his girlfriend drank beer.

'So, you give your girlfriend beer to drink, bafanas?' the man asked Thami with wide eyes.

'No, I don't, ntate,' he replied.

'So, you leave her to drink by herself? What about you then?'

'I don't drink, ntate.'

'Are you sure?' he asked Thami.

'Yes, I'm completely sure.'

The cop pulled out his handkerchief, took off his cap and again helped himself to Thami's mirror, mopping off the accumulated sweat. As he fixed his cap back onto his head, he told Thami, 'It's so nice to be a child of Mandela. You eat all sorts of cheese at home, your girlfriends drink beer and you see black boys driving Ford Fiestas, who fuck their women to the point of passing out.' The man laughed loudly and Thami was forced to share an awkward laugh with him.

'So, tell me, child of Mandela, do you know the strength of the sun? What am I saying? Of course not, Ford Fiestas come with an air conditioner. You don't even have to make your own meals! You wake up and zip straight to a place where the hands will make your food. I have no doubt that there'll be more drinking at that table. Anyway, even if you don't know the feel of the heat, I'm sure you can see its effects.' He paused. Thami was waiting for him to finish.

'So, don't you want to help the less fortunate, forced to work in this relentless heat, if only to get an umbrella?'

There it was. The moment the entire conversation had been leading up to. For the first time, Thami noticed that the Polo had parked a little further down the road, waiting for them. Thami shifted uncomfortably and decided that he wanted to end the inconvenience as soon as possible.

'How much do umbrellas go for these days?' he asked.

The cop had a hint of a smile on his lips with his elbow now resting on Thami's window. He carelessly looked into the distance, pretending he hadn't heard

Thami's question. He turned to look at him.

'Take out your licence, put a hundred note at the back of it and then hand me the licence. I'll use the hundred to buy an umbrella,' he instructed.

Thami obeyed.

The cop made his way to check the licence disk on the car's windshield. He tucked the money into his pocket as he bent over to inspect the disk. He walked back to Thami's window, chuckling to himself. He glanced at Thami's licence for a while longer before giving it back to him.

'Sho, child of Mandela, who fucks coloured girls, drives a Ford Fiesta and gives money away for free.' The cop continued chuckling at him. Thami looked at him, bemused. 'Go on, son of Mandela, your breakfast must be getting cold by now.'

Thami watched him walk away in his rear-view mirror. He turned when he heard the hoot from the Polo. As he took off, Nthabiseng stirred. She opened her eyes and looked at him with a sleepy smile.

'Are we there yet?' she asked.

'Almost,' he replied, returning her smile.

'Wake me up when we get there, Thami,' she sang softly and went back to sleep.

Thami felt a flutter of yellow butterflies in his stomach from the way she said his name. He wondered if she really understood just how much he liked her. Before his thoughts could linger, he had a flashback to the interaction with the policeman. How did he allow himself to be hustled like that, for absolutely no reason?

He drove up the ramp of Pretoria's favourite mall and breathed a sigh of relief when they were able to find parking easily at the entrance nearest the Wimpy. His thoughts had cleared entirely as he parked and fumbled to take off his seatbelt. He tapped Nthabiseng on the shoulder, waking her. She opened her eyes again with the same smile and gently asked, 'We here yet?'

'We are,' he confirmed.

'Great! Cause I really, really need to pee,' she told him.

They walked into the Wimpy together. Nthabiseng spotted her friends, already seated.

'Why don't you go join them?' The pressure on her bladder was becoming intolerable. Thami looked at her. 'They won't eat you,' she said as she bee-lined for the bathroom, leaving him standing at the entrance. She entered the bathroom and the first available cubicle. With both hands on either side of the stall, she sighed gently as she felt the relief. As the rush soothed to a trickle, she suddenly remembered that she still hadn't gotten back to her mother. She found her phone in her pocket, took it out and switched it off aeroplane mode. She saw that her mother had tried to call twice and that there was a two-minute voice message for her to listen to. She took her earphones out of her pocket and listened to her mother's message.

> 'Baby, what's going on? Why haven't you been able to reply to a single message? I just keep seeing that you've received the messages, which means you're reading them but rudely not replying. What's happening kgante? uLinda told me that you have friends staying over and you know that is fine, but you should at least inform us. Ha eh ausi, this is simply not on.'

Nthabiseng stared at the phone with no emotion. She realised how hot and thirsty she felt and regretted not asking Thami to order her a beer. She returned her focus to the phone and thought about what she wanted to write, before allowing her thumbs to glide across the keyboard.

> 'Hey Mum, I'm sorry for not replying to your messages. I guess I got a little swept up in socialising. Joan, Tumi and Monique came over. The guys also came for a little, the house is still standing, I promise. I love you Mum, please also send Papa my love. When do you guys get back? Miss you!'

She sent the message. She washed her hands, splashed a bit of water on her face and went to join the table.

On her approach, she noted that everyone seemed to be focused on Thami. Tumi cast her a smile that she felt was trying to tell her something. Thami had managed to get himself a seat at one end of the table, where he was forced to face Pieter on the other end. Monique sat to his left and Siya to his right. Tumi was in between Siya and Joan. Jason was next to Pieter, which left space for Nthabiseng between Monique and Jason. She pulled out her chair and took her place.

'I guess he was looking for some sort of bribe,' Thami finished upon her arrival. He looked to her in a panic, as if expecting her to help him with the next appropriate social cue. Or maybe he wanted her to take the attention off him. Everyone turned their gaze on her, with half smiles. She took in all their glossy red eyes, messy hair and wrinkled clothing. Everyone at the table looked rough, except for Thami.

'I'm not sure if I'm just smelling my own pits and breath, but I have a feeling we as a unit might not smell like a bed of roses at the moment,' she said to the table.

They continued smiling at her.

Monique finally turned to Thami and asked, 'So where was she,' she flicked her head at Nthabiseng, 'during all this drama?'

'Um ...' Thami shifted uncomfortably in his seat.

'Wait ...' Nthabiseng started, looking around at everyone at the table. She furrowed her brow and they all looked at her with expectant eyes. Thami still seemed to be pleading with her with his eyes. 'Am I the only person at this table who's going to have a drink? Also, where's the waiter?' Before she had a chance to say anything else, Joan's hand was raised, her fingers eagerly snapping.

'There she is!' she announced to the table. Nthabiseng turned to see the woman approaching from behind her.

She went straight to Joan, who said, 'Hi, sorry, my friend over there would like a drink. Do you have beer draughts?' The woman looked at her, confused for a moment. Joan repeated the question, again indicating the size with her two index fingers. The waiter confirmed and Joan pointed to Nthabiseng, forcing her to walk to that side of the table.

Nthabiseng turned to her rather clumsily, 'O kae ausi?' she said.

'Ke shap, wena?' the waitress responded, a little shocked.

'Le nna ke shap. Ke kopa draught ya Castle ausi,' Nthabiseng ordered.

Still a little taken aback, the waitress asked, 'Askies, mara o na le mengwaga e me kae, ausi?'

'Ke na le eighteen ausi.'

'Ke tlo kopa ID, tlhe.'

Everyone at the table sniggered. This often happened to Nthabiseng because she was so short and looked youngest among them. Nthabiseng shrugged her shoulders, took her ID out of her pocket and handed it to the waitress. The waitress looked at it, then gave it back to Nthabiseng.

'Hmm, okay,' she conceded, and wrote down Nthabiseng's order.

Siya ordered the same thing, and so did Jason. Pieter ordered his second brandy and Coke – to Joan's annoyance, and she clicked her tongue to let him know. He kissed her on the cheek. After repeating everyone's drink order, the waitress left. Nthabiseng looked over to Thami and lifted her eyebrows as a non-verbal check-in with him. He lifted a thumb off the table, indicating that he was fine.

Monique asked her question again, 'So, Thami, tell us again where Nthabiseng was when you were stopped at the roadblock?'

'Wait, what?' Nthabiseng asked. The table laughed at her confusion. Thami nodded at her.

'Nthabiseng, I think that's the first time I've ever heard you trying to speak a black language,' Pieter said to her. She looked back at him with a mixture of confusion and annoyance.

'Me too,' Jason added.

'I've heard her speak it a hundred times with her mom and her maid,' Joan said.

'Huh?' Nthabiseng said, looking at the three of them, then turned her head back to face Thami, 'Wait, can we focus on one thing at a time? Roadblock?'

'Yup,' Tumi said, catching her straw with her mouth and taking a sip. 'We made it straight through, but they stopped you guys,' she informed Nthabiseng while biting down on the straw.

'What?' Nthabiseng repeated to no one in particular. At that point she felt really thirsty and her skin felt a little clammy. A bead of sweat trickled down her armpit and she quashed it by tucking in her elbow. Siya smiled, focusing his eyes on her; Monique also smiled coyly next to her.

'On the way here?' Nthabiseng continued.

'Yup,' Tumi replied before Thami.

'Rather me than them, right?' he said to the table, smiling nervously, 'Considering I'm dead sober.'

'I agree,' Siya told him, lifting a fist that Thami met with his own.

'Whatever,' Tumi rolled her eyes.

'Wait, as I was sitting down you were saying that they wanted some kind of bribe ...' Nthabiseng jumped in.

Thami looked uneasy. 'Yeah the guy kept on asking all these useless questions and wouldn't shut up about the heat.'

Siya burst out laughing, 'Don't tell me he asked you for colddrink money?! I mean, my older brother and cousins have told me stories about this but I always thought they were lying!' He carried on laughing and Tumi joined him. He stretched out another fist for Thami to bump, which he did. As Nthabiseng was about to speak, the drinks arrived. The waitress placed Nthabiseng's beer in front of her first, then gave

Siya, Jason and Pieter theirs.

'Can I take your orders?' she asked.

Pieter smugly ordered the biggest breakfast available while the others settled on burgers and chips. Tumi and Siya were in a hushed conversation when Pieter asked if Siya had forgotten his wallet again, and if his sugar mommy would take care of him as always. Siya laughed it off, shaking his head at Pieter. Tumi placed the order for both of them and cast a sharp look at Pieter, who didn't notice. Nthabiseng insisted that Thami order something. He tried to protest – with the excuse of his muesli – but was shouted down. He eventually conceded to a cheeseburger and chips. She also insisted that he order a real drink. He declined and asked for a cream soda. He was booed for being a sober 'Designated Dave' by some of the others.

They all passed the plastic menus to Nthabiseng, who handed them to the waitress. 'Rea leboga ausi,' she said.

'You know, Nthabi, it surprises me sometimes when you speak a black language,' Joan said. Nthabiseng looked at her bemused. 'I'm not saying it in a bad way. I just mean it's easy to forget that you can sometimes,' she told her earnestly.

'Okay, I hardly speak much Tswana ...' Nthabiseng replied.

'Hardly? You never speak it,' Tumi announced. 'Even I find it weird at times when you choose to suddenly bust it out.'

'Yeah, that's because I don't really have much of a vocabulary,' she admitted.

'So why today?' Pieter asked.

'Why *not* today?' she asked in response.

An awkward silence fell over the table as Nthabiseng and Pieter held each other's inquisitive expressions, waiting for the other to answer the question each had posed.

'So, did you buy the colddrink?' Siya asked Thami, to relieve the sudden tension.

Thami looked distressed from the renewed focus.

'Ja,' Pieter interjected. 'Did you play into the corruption that now runs this country?'

'Hey, wait. How do we know that this guy was actually fishing for a bribe?' Nthabiseng said. 'Maybe he was just commenting on how hot it is outside. Which it really is,' she finished.

'Ag, Nthabiseng, don't be so naive. Don't you ever read the news? You can pull up any article on Google right now about how corrupt the police are in this country. They'll do anything for a buck, those pigs,' Pieter shot back.

As she opened her mouth to respond, the waitress returned with their meals. 'Rea leboga ausi,' she told the waitress.

'There's another one!' Jason shouted. Everyone at the table laughed except for Monique and Nthabiseng.

'I'm not saying that police aren't corrupt. I'm just saying that I don't think it's fair to suddenly label *all* police as corrupt,' Nthabiseng clarified. She looked to Thami for support but found him staring at his plate, taking a bite of his burger. Pieter ignored her appeal and again asked Thami if he had played into the hands of corruption.

'Wait, that question answers itself. He didn't do anything so there was no reason for him to pay for a bribe,' Monique told Pieter. Pieter looked at Thami, who was still focused on his burger. Nthabiseng also took a moment to watch him as she took a sip from her beer.

During the meal she stepped out of the restaurant to take a call from her brother.

'Hey,' she said into the phone.

'Yo, your mom's blowing up my phone looking for you,' Xolani began.

'Nice greeting.'

'Just stop trying to give Mom a heart attack, otherwise they're going to force me to start babysitting,' he said.

'Yeah, sorry. I did mean to get back to her, but I've been at it since, like, seven last night.'

'Whatever, just get ahold of her so she can stop stressing me,'

'Don't worry, Xoli, I've already sent a message,' she replied.

'Cool.'

'Is that all you called for?'

'What else would you like to talk about?' he returned.

'Ouch, okay.'

'I'm joking. What you getting up to today?'

'Not really sure. We decided to grab a Wimpy breakfast but don't have anything planned otherwise.'

'G called me this morning, inviting us over this afternoon for a pool party braai vibe or whatever …'

'Who's G?'

'Gangisizwe and Nonkululeko, dude.'

'Oh … oooh! Holy fuck, that's random! We haven't seen those people in like—'

'Forever. I know. He just called me out of nowhere this morning, telling me to come through with you and that we could bring whoever we wanted.'

'Holy shit. Okay, um … what should we bring or not bring there?'

'He was all like not to bring anything cause he's got it all covered. But I don't know, I would feel a bit weird to rock up empty handed, so just buy some booze and meat.'

'You sure it'll be okay if I bring my friends? Won't it be a bit weird?'

'It sounds like he's trying to have a party, so I'm sure it'll be chilled. I'll send you the address. Last night was rough; me and Bell need some time to become human again, so we'll probably head through at around, like, three this afternoon.'

'Cool, I'll see what these guys say. Oh yeah, and Thami's coming too,' she tried to rush through the last part of the sentence.

'Who's that?' he asked.

'That photographer guy from school I told you about,' she said through gritted teeth.

'The weird one?'

'Well, I don't think he's really weird.'

'Well, okay, guess I'll judge for myself. I'll meet you guys there.'

'Don't you want to buy the meat and booze for us?' she whined into the phone.

'Bye.'

'Okay, wait …'

'What?'

'Whose house am I going to tell the guys we're going to?'

'They'll figure it out at some point; it's not like he's shy about announcing to the world who he is.'

'So why do you want to go?'

'Look, dude, you don't have to come if you don't want to.'

'I didn't say that.'

'Okay, then I'll see you there. I'm trying to go back to sleep. Bye.'

He dropped the call. She had been standing against

the railing at the restaurant's entrance, absentmindedly looking down at the mall traffic. Watching people walking into retail stores and up and down the escalators. For the first time she noticed how out of place they all were. She looked around at the people busying themselves around her. Parents with their children, couples shopping together and a few early teens dressed to the nines for a day hanging out at the mall with their friends. She took in the number of families dining around them in the restaurant and registered all the eyes tracking her return to the table. She took a sip of beer and scanned the number of tables that seemed uncomfortable with theirs. There were constant shifting glances being tossed at them. The whispers around them could almost be heard. Some people stared with open hostility, while others seemed more curious.

As she looked around, she landed on a pair of pale-green eyes. Nthabiseng smiled at their owner, who returned her smile. The salt-and-pepper moustache keeping the pair of eyes company seemed intensely disturbed by the exchange. For the first time, she noticed that they were in a hostile environment. They weren't in any imminent danger, but it was evident from the atmosphere that they were an unwanted element.

She looked over to Jason, Joan and Pieter who were joking with each other, none the wiser. Monique and Tumi were on their phones; Siya and Thami looked like they had found something to talk about. She felt a little dizzy and short of breath. She thought about telling someone but didn't know what she'd say if someone did lend her an ear. She decided to take a huge gulp from the beer in front of her, which was half full, and burped loud enough to attract the direct attention of the other tables. She smiled widely and shrugged.

'Jesus! It smells like beer!' Joan exclaimed and they all laughed.

'I suggest we get the fuck out of here!' Nthabiseng announced to the table.

'I agree,' Monique said, 'I need to shower and get some fucking sleep.'

'Sleep for what? For who?' she asked Monique. 'My brother just called and invited us to a pool party where I promise we'll be well taken care of.'

'We're in!' Pieter said, speaking for himself and Joan. Joan looked taken aback by the sudden declaration. She looked at Nthabiseng, blushed slightly and nodded. Tumi, Siya and Jason concurred.

'I think I'd rather just go home,' Monique told Nthabiseng. 'I don't think I'm up to it.' She seemed sincere.

Nthabiseng wasn't going to let her off the hook, though. 'No way. Unless everyone at this table right now commits to this plan, it won't happen for anyone!' she declared. 'That includes you.' She looked directly at Thami. Siya started singing and drumming a beat on the table.

'Come on! Come on! Come on! Come on! Come on!' They all cheered on to convince Monique and Thami. The noise disrupted the other patrons and convinced the last members of the crew to join the quest. After Joan insisted that their waitress take a picture of the squad for the 'gram, they called for the bill, all rapidly beating the table with their hands. The other patrons stared in disbelief at the boorish mass accosting their breakfast peace. As they paid the bill, Nthabiseng relished the animosity the air carried in the restaurant. She looked around, deliberately wanting to make eye contact with every one of the other guests. The last pair of eyes she landed on were the pale greens from earlier. While the moustache that sat across from her quivered red, almost at the point of bursting a vein, the pale greens smiled knowingly. There was a hint of nostalgic recognition of what drove the raucous crew's behaviour. Nthabiseng too smiled knowingly, as she walked out of the Wimpy.

## WISDOM

*Betrayed by The Fish and their own children, The Children were never afforded the opportunity to subject themselves to the process of underwater evolution. Instead, The Fish built large air-bubble containers that were reserved for The Children. It was there that*

*they remained. Their only purpose was to be ogled at as strange creatures from above. This was a fate they would never escape. It came to be that with each passing generation, their tale of origin became a myth amongst themselves that served the futility of hope.*

*The silence that swept across them was slow in initiation. Some say that the silence that befell The Children was inevitable. Others say that it was orchestrated. Without speakers to confirm, the reason will never be known. It happened without notice. When they stopped speaking, their tongues served no purpose, and so it came to pass that their removal from the land gave rise to the evolution they had first sought. Only, it came in the form of shrinking tongues that eventually disappeared. Beneath that sea they forgot the existence of the sky and only felt the water's pressure, never fully understanding why.*

*Even if The Children were to grow their tongues again, what language would they be likely to speak? Would it not be an incomprehensible gibberish that would be accompanied by their inability to listen?*

\*

'So, who's this G guy? I've never heard you talk about him,' Bell turned towards Xolani. 'He's kind of a family friend. His dad and my uncle were in exile together,' he told her casually, as they opened the doors to his car and got inside.

'I think it's so cool that your uncle fought against apartheid. It's pretty crazy,' she said.

'I guess,' he shrugged as he started the car and reversed out of the gate to her complex.

They both waved to the security guard as they drove off.

'So, what's he doing at the moment?'

'To be honest, I have no idea. I haven't seen the guy since, like, matric. We were never really close, so this is a bit random.'

'So, why'd you say yes?'

'I don't know. We weren't doing anything else today. Figured that some time by the pool would be a bit of fun?'

'I'm not complaining, but you just don't seem that excited about seeing this guy. Especially after such a long time.'

She put her hand on his knee. When he pulled up to the red robot he turned to look at her and shrugged. He was irritated by the heat and couldn't think straight.

Bell decided to change the topic and asked him where they were going.

'Pretty close to Arcadia,' he told her.

Bell was also feeling a bit fragile from the previous night and decided not to pursue conversation. She plugged the audio jack into her phone and decided to play music rather than sit in the moody silence. She took note of the route and thought about how seldom she drove into the city. The trees arched over the roads, which were covered in a blanket of purple petals that fell from the jacarandas. She watched the Union Buildings come into view as they drove down the road; the site of the presidential seat of power. She observed a passing thought of how easy it was to forget that they lived in the nation's capital. She noticed the street activity beginning to thin, as they turned off into more residential-looking areas. They passed a number of street signs that indicated that the area had limited access.

'I've never been to this side of town before,' she told Xolani.

'Yeah,' he said turning down the volume of the music slightly. 'It's not that popular out here.'

They drove for some time down a narrow street ending in what looked like a very large gated housing estate. There was a guardhouse at the entrance, which they pulled up to. Two policemen stepped out and made their way to the car. One of them held an instrument Bell first thought was gun, but then realised was a metal stick of some kind with mirrors attached to the bottom.

She turned to Xolani, confused. 'I don't think we're at the right place.'

'Um ... yeah. We are,' he replied without much

feeling. He rolled down his window and spoke to the officer at his door, while the other poked the stick with the mirrors under the car and then walked around it.

*

Thami reluctantly left his car at Nthabiseng's house and found himself in the back seat of the shuttle service she had called; she and her friends were playing their favourite rap hits of the year. He wasn't moved by the commercial songs that blared out of the corner speaker he was sitting next to. He still didn't like her friends very much. He thought of them as selfish and entitled. The kind of people who got away with anything and everything because their parents spoilt them, and teachers found them charming for some or other reason. They all seemed oblivious to anything that wasn't in their world of comfort. The rugby guy, Siya, had taken it upon himself to be the one to keep him company in the back seat and sat between Tumi and Thami. Nthabiseng sat in the passenger seat with her phone, in control of the music. The driver didn't seem to be too bothered by the noise that the group was making, or by the fact that they had open beers that they were all drinking.

Siya had the trying habit of putting his arm around Thami's neck and pulling him closer to sing gibberish in his ear that barely resembled the words of the song he was trying to rap along to. Thami had to endure the awkward journey by constantly pulling himself out of Siya's grip and figured out that he could use his camera as a buffer from the ordeal. He pretended to be taking pictures of the festive mood in the vehicle but was soon forced to take real pictures when Nthabiseng and her friends started posing for the camera.

Tumi reached over from the other side, snatching the camera from him and insisting that he also needed to be in a picture. Siya took another opportunity to put his arm around him and posed for the picture. Thami was disappointed that he had allowed himself to end up in such an anxiety-inducing situation.

'Dude, relax!' shouted Siya's beer breath at Thami over the noise as he took his camera back the moment Tumi had taken the picture. 'Have a sip.'

'I don't drink!' Thami shouted back with a thumbs up.

'That's okay! You're going to drink at some point today, so why not start now?'

Thami shook his head and smiled and tried to look out the window. He felt the weight of Siya's arm around him again, increasing the pressure that he was now forced to endure.

'Come on, bru!'

He silently bemoaned not having found a way out of being around Nthabiseng's friends. He felt Siya wriggle him in his large bicep another time and turned, took a sip of the beer and then handed it back to him. Siya cheered and clapped, as did Tumi beside him. He called for the attention of the rest of the passengers and Nthabiseng turned the volume of the music down. Thami hated the attention and the bitter taste of beer in his mouth felt like a stain. It was the only word he could come up with to describe it.

'Thami has just had his first sip of beer!' Siya announced to the van. Everyone cheered and hollered.

'Finally!' Pieter shouted out, 'I was beginning to think you're gay!'

Everyone laughed.

Thami himself gave a feeble laugh. Nthabiseng dedicated the next song to him. It was by Wiz Khalifa, one of the new rappers he hadn't taken the time to listen to, featuring Snoop Dogg. 'Young, Wild and Free' had one of those easy-to-catch choruses and the usual bubblegum happy-go-lucky melody and bounciness for a summertime beat. As if trying to change his view on their taste in music, the group decided to sing the song at the top of their lungs, directly at him, pointing at him and each offering him a sip of their drink after each line. Nthabiseng had turned around in her seat, smiling and singing at him. He hadn't released the can he had opened when he took the first sip from Siya and wiped his mouth with the back of his hand after each sip. He suddenly found himself starting to sing along to the catchy chorus, to the delight of those in the van. He gave in to the atmosphere and decided to let go.

The song was played on repeat and as they pulled up to the entrance, Nthabiseng turned down the volume and announced to the van, 'Welcome to the presidential compound; be cool.'

She stepped out and walked to meet the policemen making their way to the car. The others watched and laughed at what she had just said, but were confused by the policeman who had been circling the car moving a mirrored instrument beneath it. Monique was the only person in the car who knew that Nthabiseng was not joking. Nthabiseng got back into the car and the gates swung open. The driver nervously edged through to the driving path and lifted a stiff hand to greet the policemen.

'Um ... Nthabi,' Joan broke the stupefied silence that had suddenly befallen the car. 'Where are we?'

Monique answered, 'She wasn't kidding at the gate.'

Silence fell in the car, as everyone took in the vast lawns and some of the houses on the property. The path leading up to the massive house on top of the hill was completely shaded by the enormous tree overhead. As the car pulled up to the entrance of the house, Nthabiseng caught sight of her brother's car, which comforted her a bit. The number of cars in the lot was more than she had anticipated. She hadn't thought that the party was going to be this big. She climbed out of the car first and Monique slid open her door and jumped out with her. They looked at each other nervously, not knowing what to expect. Pieter, Siya and Jason each lifted a case of beer out of the car and followed Nthabiseng and Monique up the stairs into the house. Thami stood at the entrance and looked at the double-storey house's high ceilings, chandeliers and marble floors before following the music and noise like the others.

The hallway they walked through was an archive of pivotal moments in the South African revolutionary struggle and its transition to democracy: from political rallies to mugshots of the party's most prominent and wanted leaders. Moments were captured from the military camps, the table negotiations to shape the future democracy and the transitional, celebratory, punch-drunk love photos of diverse embraces and unity. It was a surreal tunnel of time to emerge from into the lively kitchen.

'You have crossed the line that capriciously separates the rich from the entitled ...' someone called from the patio outside the open sliding kitchen door. 'Act accordingly!' he finished. His skin was more yellow than brown, tightly wrapped around his angular face. For some reason, the indentation on his chin seemed to match his voice and disposition. He was the kind of person who wore a waistcoat without irony. He bit down on the end of his tobacco pipe as he spoke, and held a whiskey tumbler in one hand. His face was more satisfied than smug. His light brown eyes studied everyone they fell on, intent on stripping them of their social inventions.

After tapping the pipe a few times, emptying its burnt contents, he gently placed it on the table that he sat at the head of, with a few of the other guests, who included Bell and Xolani. The guests took the newcomers in as he got up and made a show of his six-foot-five height and wiry frame. Arms spread, he headed straight for Nthabiseng who caught the embrace with her head landing just below his chest.

'Why has it taken so long for us to reunite?' he asked her.

'We don't exactly move in your circles, do we?' she replied.

'Well, that's a bit false. I see Uncle Zweli much more often than I get to spend time with you and your brother. It's almost as if it's on purpose.' He finally let her go. 'Knowing that you and my sister are the exact same age is a bit baffling. Last time I saw you, you were starting high school.'

'Where is she?'

'Down at the pool.' He looked past Nthabiseng and noticed Monique. 'Another face I recognise!' Monique was also enveloped in his arms and was demure interacting with him. Monique's childhood crush on him had unexpectedly endured and she was at a loss for words, seeing him for the first time since the age of fourteen. Gangisizwe took it upon himself to play the magnanimous host and graciously went about introducing himself to the rest of Nthabiseng's friends. He had a heraldic manner of speech that made him come across as more pompous than welcoming. He told all of them to make themselves at home and if they needed anything at all, not to hesitate to ask either him or his little sister, who were more than happy to serve them as their special guests. They were invited to get themselves drinks and join the table.

Bell and Xolani stood up and shared hugs with the gang, before Gangisizwe motioned for Nthabiseng and Xolani to join in the search for his little sister in order to complete the reunion of The Fantastic Four.

Nthabiseng was struck with the thought of Priscilla again, and looked at her brother accusingly. Xolani and Gangisizwe were in conversation as they made their way down the path so he missed her pointed look. It wasn't an appropriate time to bring up what she had seen on Thursday. Priscilla remained in her thoughts and she couldn't help herself from feeling sorry for her. She realised that Priscilla had for some reason carried the belief that they were still friends and she felt a pang of guilt. She recalled how they did have a friendship once, one that Nthabiseng had opted in and out of without much consideration. She considered the idea of having possibly been a spectator in Priscilla's life. How Priscilla wouldn't be the type of person – even if they had remained friends – who she would have allowed to come with her on this visit.

They descended a level of stairs and meandered through a maze of rose bushes, where a number of other guests had laid down picnic blankets and greeted them as they walked by, and then went through a white pool gate.

She looked like a starfish with her braided hair stretched out like tentacles reaching for the pool edges. She wore white Wayfarer sunglasses to complement her bikini and serenely floated on the water. It took a few calls of her name for her to stop, look over to them, gently lower her sunglasses and cast them a lazy smile. Nonkululeko stood in the centre of the pool, and languidly waded through the water and climbed up the steps. At six feet tall, her legs often became the main feature that people looked at. Still wet, she hugged the visiting sibling pair, kissing their cheeks and leaving a lingering touch of her hands on their faces.

They made small talk as she wrapped a towel around her hips and they made their way back to the patio. As they sat, she took off her glasses, greeted Nthabiseng's guests with a limp-wristed shake and gave a wet hug to Bell, who she said she was most excited to meet. It was not long before she had a grinder in her hands that she used to slowly crush her weed. As conversation continued around her, she took her time to inspect the faces around the table. She wasn't shy to look people in the eye and her gaze remained fixed on her subjects for some time before wandering off to their next target.

She was thin like her brother, a few shades darker, but with a more rounded bone structure. Where Gangisizwe's cheek bones and chin seemed to be trying to punch through the skin on his face, hers balanced on well-placed curves. They had the same pair of deep-set, light-brown eyes with a penetrating focus, with mouths that drew attention to their permanent half-smiles.

Thami had found himself at the whim of Siya, who had taken a strong liking to him. As he took in the scene unfolding around him and was being plied with alcohol, he found himself becoming increasingly distracted. Watching Nonkululeko next to her brother, observing their guests, was a surreal moment. He was in the president's home. Drinking in his home. Watching his children about to indulge in drugs. He had also been becoming increasingly uneasy with how he seemed to constantly catch Bell's eyes, although he wasn't sure who she was until Xolani returned to sit next to her. Xolani had also caught Thami's eyes several times. When Siya asked him if he wanted to go explore the grounds, he was only too happy to agree as he had felt his nervousness intensify from all the social activity at the table. Xolani watched Siya and Thami leave the table. His sister followed his eyes and he then looked directly at her.

'So, is this the new boyfriend?' he asked her in front of everyone.

Nonkululeko tapped her grinder on the table, emptying the weed into her Rizla paper. She sat between Monique and Nthabiseng and directly across from Bell. Gangisizwe was stacking his pipe at the head of the table.

'Wow,' Nthabiseng gasped, 'can you at least *pretend* to be cool though?'

'His hangover has had him a bit moody all day, don't worry about him,' Bell said to her, then kissed Xolani on the cheek. Gangisizwe smiled at the open display of affection. Xolani rolled his eyes at his sister and girlfriend.

'Maybe we should do a shot then?' Nonkululeko's calm and airy voice broke in as she licked the sticky part of the paper she'd been rolling and nimbly completed her process.

'Should we start with some Patron?' she suggested.

'Wow!' Pieter exclaimed at Joan's side, who was seated between him and Bell. 'That's that really expensive tequila, neh?' he grinned widely, waiting for a response that was given with conspiratorial smiles and darting eyes that made surreptitious contact around the table. Tumi, who sat next to him, rolled her eyes for Monique to see.

The silence was broken by Ayanda, one of the other guests, who sniggered while blurting out, 'Iphumaphi lentwana?' giving those who understood reason to snicker to themselves. Nthabiseng and Xolani shared a knowing smirk.

Nonkululeko broke the awkward moment by politely standing over the table – joint in mouth – and filling the shot glasses that patiently awaited her in the centre. With her hand occupied, she craned her neck towards Nthabiseng who gingerly pried the burning member from her lips and placed it between her own. While releasing a thin vapour of smoke, Nonkululeko elegantly handed all the guests seated at the table their share of her offerings.

'Salut!' she cheered softly, her arm stretched toward the middle of the group.

'Salut!' they all chorused.

Nthabiseng passed the joint on to Monique, who took a single drag before passing it on to Jason who sat next to her. The joint seemed to be the focus of the table as it made its way around the gathering. Everyone watched its rotation from fingertip to mouth, mouth to fingers, fingers to mouth again. By the time it reached Xolani there was only a single drag left. He looked to Gangisizwe, who gave a friendly nod before he took the final inhale and completed everyone's introduction to one another.

*

In the rose garden, Siya and Thami had found themselves in the company of the other guests who had decided to rather set up a picnic than sit inside. They had been only too happy to invite the aimlessly wandering pair over. It was initially a relief for Thami, who was still unsure of how it came to be that he and Siya were bound together, and what conversation they could possibly maintain amongst themselves. Siya had remained enthusiastic about Thami taking sips of his beer with increasing frequency. The call from the strangers gave him reprieve from the bitter abuse of his tongue.

'Come join us!' they called, while the two of them descended the stairs from the first level of the grass lawn. Siya did not hesitate and accepted the invitation without consulting Thami, who followed him. There was a slight, unwelcome fuzz washing over him. He wasn't sure making new acquaintances was the best decision at the time, but had once again resigned himself to the whims of others. The friendly picnickers welcomed them warmly as they made space on their blanket; a predominantly blue spread, with rows of black-and-white African shields and spears lined across most of it. The guests extended their arms to each of them as they sat down. The first was Mmathabo, who wore round, diamond-studded sunglasses with Versace stamped down their sides. She was a squat figure, wearing a pair of shorts over her black, full-body swimsuit. Thabo, who sat closely next to her, was a heavy-set guy, whose shades matched Mmathabo's. He had a missing front tooth and an amiable air that his firm handshake seemed to betray. Above his glasses a bushy set of eyebrows looked like they were on course to collide in the middle of his forehead, only to come to an abrupt halt millimetres apart. Thando was the last of them. She wore a pair of blue Police aviators, revealing a small pair of eyes that looked as if they would soon be closed. Thick braids sat on her shoulders, emerging from a wide-brimmed white garden hat that shaded her face. She lay back on a pillow supported by Thabo's knee, her crossed legs covered by a lengthy pink-and-blue floral dress.

'Do you guys want a Bellini?' Thabo asked them.

'What's a Bellini?' Siya asked, before draining his beer. The trio giggled before Thando responded from her reclined position.

'It's like ...' she giggled some more and so did the other two.

'It's like a mimosa that went to private school,' Mmathabo finished for her. Thami was lost by the conversation but awkwardly giggled with the trio and Siya, who seemed to be just as tickled as the rest of them.

'How is that even possible?' Siya asked.

They all continued to laugh.

'Nxa! This is why I don't like hanging around peasants,' Thando joked. 'I even had to teach these two about the finer things in life. I need classier friends,' she said pointing at her two companions. Their laughter increased as Thami forced out his own.

'Tsek, jou swine!' Mmathabo blurted through her giggles.

'Okay, this sounds amazing! Can we please have some?' Siya requested without consulting Thami, who tried to decline politely. Thabo pulled his shades down his nose a bit and told Thami that he'd absolutely love it. Thami felt it would be rude to decline a second time and hesitantly accepted the offer. Siya smiled at him from behind his sunglasses, before asking the group the difference between a mimosa and a Bellini. They watched Thabo reach into a picnic basket to pull out flute glasses and juice.

'Madame! Our new guests would like to be cultured; can you please respond,' Mmathabo said to Thando, who looked out at the descending levels on the enormous grounds they were in. At the far end of the gardens, they could see a thick forest of purple and green with the city buildings littered beyond them.

'Well,' she said with an exaggerated sigh, 'what was the point of educating you, if you can't then use that to teach others?'

'You're so full shit! You know that?' Mmathabo told Thando.

They all chuckled.

'Well,' Mmathabo started, 'according to Miss Madame over here, what makes a Bellini better is that it's not as common.' She paused to share a giggle with Thabo. 'Mara they're the same vele; they just have different names, like Jason and Jared.' They all laughed at this and Thando decided to take back the conversation.

'Listen, darlings,' she sounded out her vowels with an embellished polishing, 'a mimosa is made with Champagne, a sparkling wine bottled in France, and mixed with orange juice. While a Bellini is made using Prosecco, a sparkling wine bottled in Italy, and is mixed with a peach purée,' she finished, holding an extended note of the vowels of her last word, as she had before. Thabo handed Siya and Thami their flutes.

'So, what you guys are saying is, if I mix JC Le Roux with Oros, I'll have a ghetto-rich drink that I can name?' Siya said.

They all roared with laughter. Mmathabo slapped Siya on the shoulder and Thando found herself spilling her own drink as she turned on her side to laugh. Thami took the opportunity to offer her his and she waved him off and lifted her glass above her head for Thabo the barman to work for her. Thabo smiled, shaking his head.

'Magic words …' he said with one side of his nearly single eyebrow raised.

'Thabo Gcabashe is the world's greatest lover and could spread me like Aids through Africa,' Thando sighed.

'Thank you,' he said sweetly and took her glass.

They looked at the shocked pair with increasing fits of giggles before they all boomed into another round of laughter.

'So, what do you guys do?' Mmathabo asked Siya and Thami as they took their first sips. Thami loved the sweet taste and was excited that he couldn't taste any alcohol.

'Wow! This tastes so good!' he said to everyone. They gave him a knowing smile.

Siya slapped him on the back. 'Finally!' he shouted. 'I've been trying to get him to drink the whole day and he's been taking sips like a little girl,' he told the others.

'Cause I don't drink,' Thami said frankly.

'You do now,' Thando said without looking at him. Thami smiled shyly at her profile.

'Oh, shut up, wena!' Thabo told her jokingly. 'What do you guys do? You look like first-years.'

'We're actually matrics,' Siya told him.

Mmathabo, Thando and Thabo gave a collective gasp.

'No way! So, are you guys Nkuli's friends?' Mmathabo asked.

'Yeah, trust her to bring us such cute jailbait,' Thabo said.

'Hayi, wena!' Mmathabo said, slapping his knee.

Siya and Thami exchanged awkward looks and tried to laugh off the comments.

'Um ... we're actually Nthabiseng's friends,' Siya told them.

'Who's Nthabiseng now?' Thando asked frowning at them.

'Um ... Xolani's sister?' he tried; they all still seemed confused. 'They're friends with the family,' he added.

'Xolani ...' Mmathabo said pensively. 'Why does that name sound familiar?'

'He's that guy in that band isn't it? His sister is coloured, right?' asked Thando.

'Oooh, them!' Thabo said.

'Oooh,' Mmabatho repeated. 'I remember them! His band has been doing kinda well hasn't it?'

'Yeah!' Siya excitedly told them. 'You should see them live! We went to their last show on Thursday. It was pretty fucking cool!'

'So you have the kind of parents who let you out on a school night, vele?' Mmathabo looked from Siya to Thami in shock.

'Not really.' Siya bashfully toned down his

animation and admitted that he had lied to his parents about a school rugby dinner he was expected to attend as the first-team captain.

'At least we know what those calf muscles are for now,' Thabo said, and pointed to Siya's legs, in shorts that cut off just above his knees. 'And wena, what was your excuse?' he asked Thami.

'I wasn't there,' Thami admitted. He tried to take another sip from his glass, only to realise that it was empty. He felt silly over having done that, and self-conscious about his desire to ask for more. He resolved to place the glass somewhere beside him but was intercepted by Thabo's arm reaching for the flute, a pleasing gesture.

'So, what do you guys plan on doing next year?' Thando asked them, breaking off Thami's concentration from watching a new drink being poured for him. He saw that Thando had turned her head to face them and was looking at him with a smile.

'Well,' Siya started, stealing Thando's attention, as Thabo handed Thami his freshly topped-up flute.

'Pretend you're used to these nice things and sip it slowly this time. I promise we've got enough,' Thabo told Thami, who smiled at him with embarrassment.

'I don't really know yet. But I'm thinking of doing sports science at Tuks,' Siya told them. The triad conspiratorially avoided eye contact with each other and just smiled into their flutes mockingly, unenthused by his lack of academic ambition.

'That sounds really ... interesting,' Mmathabo said to him. 'What about you, Thami?'

'Um ...' Thami thought to himself as he looked out at the gardens below, and the city beyond. 'I don't know yet,' he shrugged. He turned to look at everyone and smiled. 'I kind of just want to take my car and road trip by myself around the country.' They all went silent and looked at him questioningly for a moment before convulsing with laughter.

'What the fuck?!' Thabo exclaimed. 'That is the whitest boy shit I've ever heard anyone say!' Everyone continued to laugh.

'Are you being serious? You're not being serious, are you? Are you being serious?' Thando snorted between laughs. Everyone on the blanket couldn't stop laughing at the thought and Thami was forced to chuckle along with them.

'Yeah, I'm serious.' He watched them all laugh at him.

'Wait, how? Why? For what?' Siya asked, genuinely puzzled.

'I just want to travel the country and take pictures wherever I go,' he replied earnestly.

'Oh, sweetie,' Mmathabo said with a tone of concern, 'were you one of those black kids who went to school without shoes by choice?'

They all shrieked with laughter again. Thami also

began to laugh at himself and realised how ridiculous his intended adventure sounded on hearing himself telling people about it for the first time.

'Seriously, though, please don't do that. Our country is so dangerous and if you think Pretoria's whites are bad, what do you think the feral ones out there are going to be like?' Mmathabo continued.

'Mara what were you going to be doing on this trip?' Thabo sniggered.

'Take photos,' Thami smiled lazily. 'Wait, where's my camera?' he asked, looking around him, suddenly realising that he did not have it.

'Relax, Thami,' Siya told him. 'You left it at the table. I doubt it'll get stolen at the president's house.' He then turned to his new friends and asked them how they knew the president's kids.

'You don't need to keep saying the word "president". I think we all know where we are by now,' Thabo told him with a smile.

'Ignore him,' Thando said. 'We all grew up together; our parents are all friends,' she finished her sentence and raised her glass to be refilled.

'Magic words ...' Thabo said.

'Voetsek! Just fill my glass, wena!' she told him.

'You're lucky I like you, wena,' he told her as he took the glass.

'Does that mean that all your parents also, like ... work for the government?' Thami asked them.

'What a boring question,' Thando said.

'It really is,' Thabo agreed. 'Mmathabo, don't you want to roll us something nice there?'

'Hawu, why I must I do it?' Mmathabo asked him.

'Because you're the only delinquent here who can,' he told her, while handing over Thando's glass.

'You know that Madame here is useless, I'm playing barman la, and I don't trust the jailbait.'

'Fine!' she conceded and started preparing the first joint Thami would ever smoke, with some encouragement from Thando.

\*

'So, I just asked her; what could possibly be more British than America's complete thirst for global occupation, aside from Asian tea of course?' Gangisizwe dropped his final punchline for the table. Everyone laughed politely as he surveyed the gathering. Monique looked away almost immediately when his smile landed on her. Nthabiseng stood at the braai stand that was built into the wall just outside the kitchen, allowing her to observe and participate from a short distance.

She had to contend with Ayanda over the right to start the fire. It was a well-mannered conversation, in which he had sceptically questioned her fire-making prowess, to which she responded that she had boer blood running through her veins. He acquiesced to assuming a supervisory role. She told him that she'd allow him to cook the meat and requested that he marinate it. He accepted his delegated role with a forced humility. A fourth joint had been making its way around the table. Her stationing at the fire gave her reprieve from the one that seemed to never stop burning at the table. She asked Joan for a cigarette, who moaned that Nthabiseng never bought her own and always smoked hers.

'But you know I only smoke when I drink. I'm not like an actual smoker,' she told her friend.

'Then you should buy your own when you drink,' Joan told her as she got up and joined her at the fire.

'So, you're one of those annoying people who finishes everyone's cigarettes at the party, but doesn't really smoke,' Nonkululeko called over the table, while passing the latest joint over the empty chair Nthabiseng had left, to Monique who immediately gave the joint on to Jason and Tumi. Nonkululeko grabbed her cigarette box off the table and wafted over to Nthabiseng and Joan.

'Here,' she said to the pair. 'Put those away; you absolutely have to try these,' she offered her box to each of them to take out a stick.

'I'm joining you guys,' Xolani said. He got up just as Bell received the joint from Pieter.

'Sure,' Nonkululeko said with a soft excitement. 'So, I get these from this German guy I go to school with and I promise you'll never want to smoke anything else once you try them.' She lit all their cigarettes for them. They all raised their eyebrows after their first drag and exhaled with delight. 'What did I tell you?' she smiled confidently. Joan, Nthabiseng and Xolani all inspected their cigarettes as if it was a coordinated effort.

'This is fucking amazing,' Xolani said. 'Like, I can feel all the fluffiness in my mouth, but it hits the back of my throat so smoothly, but I can also still, like, feel it at the same time. If that makes any sense.'

'I completely get what you're saying,' Joan added. 'It also has such a nice taste, like it almost tastes like peanuts,' she said, then backtracked. 'Actually, now I just sound like a fucking idiot.'

'No, not at all,' Nonkululeko's slow and tranquil voice reassured her. 'That's how it tastes.' She shared a reassuring smile with Joan.

'This is just fucking amazing,' Nthabiseng added as her contribution to the conversation.

'Great! I'm so glad you like them. Unfortunately, I didn't bring that many back home with me from school, but I'll give you guys a box each later if that's okay.'

They all looked at her in amazement and accepted the offer, telling her that it was more than enough.

'I'll bring more home with me next time to share with you guys,' she said.

They awkwardly thanked her for her generosity and fell into a silence, looking into Nthabiseng's fire.

'That's a pretty good-looking fire you've got going there, kid,' Xolani told Nthabiseng, while putting an arm around her shoulder.

'Thanks,' she said, and put her arms around his waist. 'Why were you in such a mood earlier?'

'Fuck, I don't know. I've gone in pretty hard the last three days. Sorry for snapping at you on the phone earlier.'

'It's cool.' She suddenly remembered something and let go of her brother to reach for her phone on the table. 'I should send Mama a message just to keep up communication.'

'Good idea,' he told her.

Joan and Nonkululeko observed the pair as a silent audience.

'I'm just gana go to the bathroom. I'll send her a WhatsApp from there,' she informed him as she chucked the remainder of her cigarette into the fire.

'I'll come with you,' Joan said and followed her, leaving Nonkululeko and Xolani as the sole guardians of the fire.

'Nkuli,' he said, smiling at her.

'Xoli,' she said, smiling back.

He couldn't think of anything meaningful to say, so he threw his cigarette butt into the fire and asked her if she wanted to return to the table. He accepted her being fine by the fire and thanked her again for the cigarette before taking his place between Bell and Gangisizwe.

'It's so cool to be here and to just hang out like this,' Pieter said, as Gangisizwe poured more shots for the table. He smiled at Pieter.

'Yeah, it's so chilled,' Tumi added. 'Thank you, guys, for having us,' she said, looking at Nonkululeko at the fire and then to Gangisizwe.

'It's our pleasure. I'm glad our childhood friends could make it. It was a spur-of-the-moment decision and we realised that we hadn't seen these guys in so long, it was becoming a sin to not check in,' he said. 'Ah! You've arrived just in time for the next round of shots,' he told Joan and Nthabiseng, who had appeared from the kitchen, followed by Ayanda, who had walked out with a tray on top of a large bowl that contained meat. Looking at Gangisizwe, Nthabiseng noticed that his skin looked to be merging with the sun's golden glow. He walked around the table to hand everyone a glass, beginning with placing a glass over Monique's shoulder, lingering a little longer than was necessary.

'Thank you,' she said through a quiet smile.

'Pleasure,' he returned into her ear at the same low volume. He placed a shot in front of everyone else at the table, including Joan who had returned to her place beside Pieter. He put four glasses on a small, circular silver tray and walked over to the braai stand.

Once everyone had a glass in hand he called 'Salut!'

'Salut!' everyone responded.

He gathered the empty glasses onto his tray and took back his place at the end of the table and began to clean his pipe in preparation for stacking it again.

'It's so easy to forget that we live in a third world country on days like this,' Pieter said, wearing a goofy grin. Gangisizwe tilted his head at the comment while unscrewing his pipe; his almost smile became slightly more pronounced. Xolani observed his actions swiftly become more deliberate.

'I agree,' Tumi said.

'Ja, it is,' Monique said wistfully.

'I've never really thought of it like that, but that kind of makes sense,' Bell added.

At the braai stand Nonkululeko wore a look of amusement; advancing her almost smile a little more to match her brother's. She made her way to the kitchen and opened the fridge.

'Would anyone like some Prosecco?' she called sweetly to the patio. There was an affirmative consensus at the table. She pulled out a few bottles and busied herself in the kitchen.

'Hmmm... What do you mean?' Gangisizwe probed.

Unsure of who was being addressed, the table went quiet for a moment. Gangisizwe knocked his pipe bowl on the ground to empty it of its charred debris. At the braai stand, Ayanda and Nthabiseng exchanged compliments on the completion of each other's respective tasks. When Gangisizwe was satisfied with his work of knocking out the residual contents of the pipe's bowl, he readjusted himself in his seat and placed the bowl on the table. As if unaware that he had disturbed the conversational flow of the table, he looked expectantly at Pieter. Behind him at the braai stand Ayanda and Nthabiseng had resolved to prepare the meat together.

'You know,' Pieter's goofy smile tried to disarm Gangisizwe's, 'South Africa is a third world country and stuff and sometimes it's just nice to forget about all that.'

Gangisizwe nodded solemnly, then absentmindedly reached into his waistcoat pocket to pull out his tobacco and pipe cleaners, placing them next to the sum of his pipe's parts. 'I guess what I'm trying to ask is: what do you mean that *you* live in a third world country?'

Pieter laughed at the question, 'What do you mean? All of us here live in a third world country.'

The others around the table joined in the laughter. Gangisizwe retrieved one of his white pipe cleaners from its packet, then looked down his disconnected pipe stem with one eye before he inserted it.

'Hmm ... I'm not sure if I agree with that,' he told Pieter.

'But most of the people in this country live like

shit. They don't have, like, toilets, they're poor, and I don't know about many first world countries that have seasons where their electricity is cut off for a few hours of every day.' Pieter tried to laugh it off.

Gangisizwe nodded again at what Pieter was saying. Everyone at the table was watching the back-and-forth, like a tennis rally picking up momentum. Gangisizwe pulled out his pipe cleaner, now coated in black and brown sludge. He placed it on the table, then pulled out another that he buried into the tube.

'I hear you,' he responded to Pieter, and contemplated him before continuing, simultaneously concentrating on his pipe cleaning. 'Do you think that you live like most people in this country do?'

Pieter was taken aback by the question. 'Of course not,' he laughed.

'So, do you understand now why I'm confused by your assertion?' Gangisizwe asked him, while examining the newly sludge-laden pipe cleaner. From the braai corner, the smell of cooking meat wafted over to where they sat. Ayanda and Nthabiseng high-fived each other, unaware of the conversation at the table.

'I hope you motherfuckers are working up an appetite cause we're making meat for days over here and it's gana be delicious! Seriously, someone should call Peta on us, there's every kind of meat you can think of burning here!' Nthabiseng called out to the table.

'We're ready!' Gangisizwe called back to her, still

focused on his pipe-cleaning efforts. Nonkululeko walked out with a tray of Champagne flutes. Joan, Monique and Tumi stood up to help clear space for the tray.

'It's so relaxed guys,' she told them. 'We just need to make enough space for me to put this down here.' By the time she placed the tray on the table, the three of them had picked up a few empty beer bottles and glasses and she told them they could put them on the kitchen counter. Then she busied herself with the weed crusher again.

'I'm sorry, but I still don't understand what you're asking me,' Pieter told Gangisizwe earnestly.

'I guess …' Gangisizwe sighed, as he pulled out his third pipe cleaner and looked at the ceiling as if searching for words to help him phrase what he was going to say next. 'I'm saying that you don't live in a third world country. None of us at this table do.'

'But what about the millions of South Africans who live in poverty?' Pieter asked him sincerely.

'Are you one of those millions?'

'No,' he acknowledged in a fluster, 'but it's not like we have perfect services either.'

'What services might you be referring to? Losing electricity every now and then? Or living without electricity in general? Or not being able to access clean running water or medical services?'

Pieter exhaled loudly to indicate his growing

frustration with the conversation, 'Well, I mean, ja, obviously load shedding is a big deal that affects the economy. And okay, I don't experience all that other stuff. But also, what about things like having to stand in Home Affairs queues forever for simple documents?' Pieter's speech was becoming increasingly spirited and slightly jumbled.

'Are you saying that all of these services used to work and now no longer do?' Gangisizwe asked, finally satisfied after pulling out a lightly stained pipe cleaner from the tube.

'Shame, I think he's just trying to say that there was a time when things looked like they were functioning smoother than they are now,' Bell tried to help Pieter out.

Nonkululeko took a moment to look up at Bell and smiled at her before she returned her focus to preparing a joint. She opened the crusher and smoothed out her rolling paper.

Gangisizwe looked at Bell and smiled. He screwed his pipe back together.

'Yeah, but my question remains, for whom were things functioning smoother before? Cause unless I've gotten my wires crossed,' he turned back to Pieter, 'and please correct me if I'm wrong, but you were saying that *we* all live in a third world country because millions of other people live in abject poverty and that sometimes even *our* basic services are interrupted, right? So, my question is, when were all these basic services running better for everyone living in this country? And how does that equate to our own lives being subject to that of the third world experience?'

He let his question hang in the air while he stacked tobacco into his pipe. Unable to answer, Bell looked at him with a mystified smile, while Xolani held an amused grin next to her and stared off into the distance. Bell was a little annoyed at his silence, as she had expected him to explain to Gangisizwe what she had meant. Instead, he left her hanging and she was frustrated at how pleased with himself Gangisizwe seemed to be. Pieter stared at him blankly and had begun to tap his fingers nervously. Those around the table exchanged confused looks. Joan and Tumi were both stunned, as was Monique. Nonkululeko and Gangisizwe simply continued with their preparations. Ayanda and Nthabiseng shared jokes at the braai stand. The smell of the meat was no longer a light, wafting scent in the air; it had matured into a strong presence coming in from the patio. The lo-fi music that had been gently playing in the background the entire afternoon suited the cooling evening light.

'Terms like "first world" and "third world" are always odd for me,' Gangisizwe suddenly picked up the conversation again. 'Cause even if it's softer language, it just means *this* place is for the whites and *this* one's for the blacks, or however else you want to characterise the rest of the world.'

Pieter resolved to revert to the cool nature he had adopted prior to the conversation. Joan had been stroking his arm and he remembered his place.

'What do you mean *this* one's for whites and *this* one's for blacks? We're white and we're here,' he offered with a renewed goofy and amiable charm, topped off with a nervous laugh. Nonkululeko had been staring off into space with the joint held up in her hand.

'Oh shit, I totally forgot to bring the actual Prosecco,' she announced to the table and laughed. They all latched onto the opportunity to enjoy the levity, however fleeting. She left the joint on the table and went back to the kitchen. She declined the offers of assistance she received from the others.

'Yeah ...' Gangisizwe returned the gathering to the conversation at hand, 'when I use terms like "first world" or whatever kak, I mean real whites, you know?'

Looks of shock fell over his guests' faces one at a time. 'Like the kind of whites who separate salt from their rice because they like to keep their whites separate.' He shrugged, struck a match and started puffing out thick plumes of smoke as he patiently started up his pipe. Once satisfied, he placed the matchstick in the ashtray in front of him.

'Yoh, now that just sounds like you're being racist,' Pieter said in an injured voice. Everyone else still had stunned expressions on their faces; they were all silently hoping for an end to the conversation.

'Dude, I'm honestly not trying to be funny or a dick,' Gangisizwe told Pieter.

Nonkululeko returned, holding a silver ice bucket in her hands. It contained four bottles.

'Yay!' Nthabiseng called from the braai stand, raising her thumbs to everyone and jumping with excitement. Tumi gave her a bemused smile and Nonkululeko returned a thumb with a wink. Monique stared at Gangisizwe with her mouth agape.

'Look, guy, I'm not being a dick about this first world thing. Honestly, think about it,' Gangisizwe continued, looking directly at Pieter, who was becoming visibly deflated, while everyone else at the table, except for Nonkululeko, seemed to be in distress. 'You call yourselves Afrikaners, right? It translates directly into Africaners. Like you know how the Irish are considered the niggers of Europe? That makes you guys the kaffirs of whiteness. Sorry man, but you shouldn't let a small thing like spelling interfere with your truth.'

The patio had been falling into increasing shadow as the springtime evening sun began its journey to the other side of the world. Bell had begun to look at Gangisizwe with open hostility, while Xolani massaged his forehead with his fingers. When Bell caught Nonkululeko's eyes smiling curiously at her, she tried to soften the glare she had been directing at her brother and blushed. She found his gall absolutely and absurdly rude but didn't know how to register her indignation adequately. Nonkululeko surveyed the rest of the perplexed faces around the table.

'Gangi, come on,' she serenely addressed her brother. 'The lights haven't even come on yet,' she said as the sensors switched on the house, patio and garden lights. Gangisizwe smiled at his sister, who rolled her eyes for the table to see. 'Enough,' she told him.

He bit down on his pipe and raised his hands in the air as if to signal surrender. Nonkululeko picked up a remote that sat on the table and turned up the sound of the lazy percussions, melancholic acoustic guitar and droning bass. She stood up, unwrapped and dramatically popped the cork off one of the bottles she had fetched.

'Whooo!' Nthabiseng shouted from outside. Ayanda whistled.

'Wow!' Tumi declared incredulously to the table.

Nonkululeko poured a glass for everyone and invited Ayanda and Nthabiseng to join in the clinking of glasses. Pieter had gotten up from his chair and seemed to be walking to the garden. Nonkululeko slyly cut him off and handed him the joint she had rolled earlier.

'According to my maths on rotation, it was your turn to light the joint. I'm, like, super superstitious, and I'll totally freak out if you don't do it,' she pleaded with him. She added another 'Please'.

Pieter grudgingly smiled at her and took the joint and lighter from her hands. She gave him a tight hug, leaning her entire frame into him, then held his face in her hands, before returning to her spot where her glass stood. Pieter went back to his place, picked up his glass and they all yelled, 'Cheers!' while making eye contact with each person they touched glasses with. Conversational chatter slowly picked up again once they sat down. The lights and increased volume of the music brought the group back to life. Monique looked at Gangisizwe with a curious contempt, which he returned with a smirk. She turned to speak to Joan, Pieter and Tumi. At the other end of the table, Gangisizwe spoke to Xolani, with Bell and Nonkululeko listening.

'Shame, little squib Draco Malfoy over there. He's all money and no power.'

Xolani indulged in a guilty chuckle with Gangisizwe and Nonkululeko.

While Bell was familiar with the reference, she sought clarity on one of its concepts.

'Wait, what's a squib?' she asked earnestly.

Gangisizwe rolled his eyes and told her, 'Someone from a magical family who can't perform magic, my muggle friend.' For the first time that day, his smile revealed the straight white teeth that his mouth held. He then turned his attention to Xolani.

Bell couldn't help the malevolent scowl that shot

out of her towards Gangisizwe. She couldn't help but feel that he was becoming increasingly antagonistic towards his guests and that, for some reason, she had made his hit list. Maybe he thought that they weren't good enough to be there. Frustrated, she thought of telling him about her liberal upbringing and how she saw the world.

She realised that Nonkululeko had been observing her face yet again, with that permanent smirk she and her brother shared. Bell was annoyed with the girl's ability to hold an unwavering stare. Nonkululeko nonchalantly smoked her cigarette as she watched her get up and excuse herself for the bathroom.

*

Thami and Siya lagged behind Mmathabo, Thabo and Thando as they made their way back to the main house. The two had volunteered to carry the picnic basket and cooler box as compensation for joining the picnic empty handed. Thami found himself laughing hysterically at almost every joke made by the others around him. He was a tad uncoordinated and zig-zagged a bit as he walked beside Siya. He felt his picnic basket connect with Siya's cooler box in minor intervals as they made their way up the garden. The other three were walking at an accelerated pace compared to Thami's stagger and step that Siya indulged. Thami abruptly stopped walking, just before they climbed the stairs and turned to Siya, who had come to a halt with him. They stood in the light-blue evening shade, listening to the distant music coming from the patio that they were headed for. Louder still were the evening crickets. Thami turned to look at the city beyond the trees they had turned their backs on. Its lights had come alive and were a sight to behold in the dusk.

'Isn't that beautiful?' Thami said with a goofy smile. 'Who knew this city could look so pretty?'

'It is pretty,' Siya chuckled, entertained by Thami's change in conduct.

'I wanted to ask you earlier,' Thami unexpectedly changed the course of conversation, 'what was that thing at the restaurant this morning?'

'What thing, man?'

'You know, when that Pieter guy was all like, "Is your sugar mommy gana pay for you again?",' he put on a deep voice and mimicked Pieter's Afrikaans accent. They both laughed at his pathetic impersonation. Thami was enjoying the light feeling of not being entirely in control of his actions. His eyelids felt heavy, but not sleepy. He felt as if they were helping him look at the world differently by shrinking it somewhat, allowing him to focus on what was immediately in front of him. When they stopped laughing, he tilted his head up to look at Siya through his slits for eyes to indicate he was expecting a response. Siya looked back at him and shook his head. He put his free hand on Thami's bald head and rubbed it a bit before answering,

'I don't know, man,' he spoke to him without making eye contact. 'It's nothing really that deep. I just don't get as much money as you guys, I guess. My parents are a little stricter than everyone else's. That's all.' He looked embarrassed by the admission.

'But,' Thami started while swaying a bit, 'and it's not like I care about this or anything like that, but aren't you, like, the first black rugby captain of our school's team?'

Siya took in a deep breath and looked at the ground before answering. 'Yeah, yeah, I am,' he finally said, with more resignation than pride.

'Well,' Thami said to Siya, looking him up and down, 'I think your friend is a bit of a cunt for saying shit like that.' Thami knew that he had possibly crossed a line, considering it was the first time he and Siya were hanging out and they weren't friends. Yet he felt confident in what he had said to Siya. After an awkward silence, they broke it by laughing together.

'I guess he kind of is,' Siya admitted. 'Now, can we get back to the braai? I'm really hungry.'

'Someone's got the munchies!' Thami sang to him in a juvenile voice, as they walked up the illuminated garden path to join the rest of the party on the patio.

They arrived to a lively line in the kitchen where people were piling food onto their plates.

'Where the fuck have you two been?' Tumi cried out to them while dishing meat onto two plates. Her cry made them the centre of attention and everyone cheered at their reappearance and insisted that they get food.

'Jesus, I even forgot that you were here! Where the fuck are you coming from?' Joan called, facing the entrance of the passage from which a sleepy Jason approached holding a hand over his eyes to shield them from the bright kitchen lights.

'I completely forgot that you were even here!' Nthabiseng exclaimed affirming Joan's proclamation.

'I went to the bathroom earlier and when I got out,' he explained in a husky whisper, 'I saw couches and sat on one, and now ... I'm, like, here.'

Everyone laughed and offered him some food. Joan also offered him a beer from the fridge, which he accepted eagerly. The hosts were the last to resume their seats, as Gangisizwe cleared the table while the others dished up and Nonkululeko prepared jugs of cucumber water with ice and clean glasses for their guests. The cucumber water was a relief that Thami hadn't anticipated he needed. He gulped down the first refreshing glass without waiting for invitation and immediately refilled it, to be consumed with dinner. Xolani's ear was the first to pick up on the striking of piano keys in a staccato rhythm. A long note held on a penny whistle and the guttural singing of a song giving instruction. As he registered the audio, he turned to look at Gangisizwe beside him. Gangisizwe gave him a knowing nod and smile.

'I like your ear, Xolani,' Gangisizwe told him.

'You make using it easy,' he replied, before they tapped their glasses and exchanged knowing glances.

Bell observed them and asked, 'Who is this?' in the same moment that Gangisizwe bit into his garlic bread. Xolani had already put a forkful of steak into his mouth and raised a hand to indicate he'd reply as soon as he was done.

'It's South African jazz musician, Zim Ngqawana,' Nthabiseng helped her out. 'Our uncle used to play us his music all the time. Uncle Zweli would never stop telling us about what an outlier he was, and how he didn't fit neatly into South African jazz definitions.' She smiled at Bell.

'Wow, it sounds really beautiful, I must say,' she responded. 'I wish I could say his name,' she joked.

'Well you can't fly unless you try,' Nonkululeko smiled at her as she picked up a potato from her plate and placed it in her mouth.

Bell laughed politely. 'You're right,' she said. 'I heard this really interesting Einstein quote somewhere, where I think he said, "If you measure a fish by its ability to climb a tree, it will live its whole life believing it's stupid.'" She smiled back at Nonkululeko, who held her polite smile.

Monique, who had also been observing the conversation, broke her day's silence.

'Uncle Zweli told us a different story,' she said. The others turned to look at her and she was suddenly shy again. Nthabiseng found her change in demeanour strikingly odd. Gangisizwe had tilted his head, eyeing her curiously. Monique smiled at him, before returning to the drumstick in her hand.

'Well, I'd definitely love to hear how Uncle Zweli and Einstein differ on the logic of fish climbing trees.' Bell held her smile politely and looked around her. Xolani pretended as if he was in deep thought and fed himself another piece of steak, embarrassed by Bell's lack of self-awareness at the table.

'Well it's, like, a really, really long story to explain, but suffice to say that our understanding of the dexterity of fish climbing trees is decidedly different to the views of Einstein,' Monique ended the conversation. 'Anyway, why are we speaking about fish? This is what happens when all we do is drink and smoke weed all afternoon. We have these weird and deep conversations.'

Everyone laughed with their hands in front of their mouths. On the other side of the table, Thami had been straining his ears to try to pick up on the conversation Nthabiseng was involved in. He called out to her over the other chatter taking place around him, to ask what the meaning of the words of the song were.

Gangisizwe answered his question for her. As he spoke, Thami noticed how he had a way of manipulating his vowels as if he were an English lord. His speech pattern distracted Thami from the content the explanation carried. Thami missed out on the fact that the song was about stick fighting, something that Xhosa boys and young men practised. The phrase being repeated throughout the song was a challenge from one boy to another, to prepare his sticks for battle. Gangisizwe had managed to recapture the entire table's attention as he had been doing the whole afternoon. By the time he had finished his explanation to a vacantly staring Thami, his only response was another question.

'Dude, has anyone ever told you that you kind of speak like Jaime Lannister?'

Everyone at the table drew in sharp breaths. Gangisizwe eyed Thami inquiringly before Nthabiseng and Xolani burst into laughter.

'Oh my God, yes!' they both said through high-pitched contagious squeals that enveloped everyone at the table. The conversation naturally flowed into a discussion about everyone's favourite characters from the world's most popular television show.

By the time they were all helping to clear the table, Siya had egged on Thami to tell the story of being harassed by the police. Thami, this time, was a lot more energetic and detailed in his account of the morning's events. The story, however, did not end up living up to the funny anecdote it was meant to be. It brought about a shift in mood. More Patron shots were taken and the music took a more lively turn.

Throughout all the activity, Ayanda, Mmathabo, Thabo and Thando drew Thami, Tumi and Siya into a discussion about playing up their privilege in moments where they found themselves accosted for no reason. Thami could barely hold the conversation; his mind was unable to concentrate on anything at that point. The taste of the last shot of Patron had remained on his tongue and he had begun to feel an unsettling nausea come over him. Without excusing himself, he quietly got up and headed straight for the bathroom where he remained, puking for a length of time he couldn't measure.

In that time the music gave birth to a dance floor. In all the merriment, Gangisizwe invited Nthabiseng and Xolani inside with the promise of showing them something only they would appreciate. When Bell had stood up to go with them, Gangisizwe politely told her that it was something only the four of them would understand. His sister was already in the kitchen, waiting for them to follow her. Xolani pecked Bell's lips, promising that they wouldn't be gone for long. He picked up his tumbler and Nthabiseng got herself a beer as she walked through the kitchen.

'Where you guys running off to now?' Thando called as they passed the dance circle that had formed near the braai stand.

'Upstairs quick. I promise to come back bearing gifts!' Gangisizwe shouted before they disappeared into the house.

'Remember how we were never allowed in here when we were kids?' Gangisizwe giggled like a naughty child, with his hand on one of the double door handles.

'When the first marriage is away ...' Nonkululeko giggled with her older brother and put her hand on the other handle. Nthabiseng and Xolani were excited themselves, because the study had always been off limits and they wanted to occupy the space as adults. Then Gangisizwe and Nonkululeko counted down to three and swung the doors open at the same time. The room that had always been referred to as a study would have been better described as a library. The wooden mahogany floors and book shelves glistened with a freshness that gave it the impression of being a rarely used space, yet fastidiously maintained. Ancient law books sat impotently undisturbed behind the glass doors of the cabinets, while others that carried with them a modern relevance were proudly stacked on meticulously fitted shelves, giving the room a circular sensibility. It boasted a staircase that led to more hidden knowledge on the next floor of the library. It was as if they were all taking it in for the first time. The room infantilised them into the children who'd been severely admonished for merely sitting on the couches where some of the country's most important decisions were made. They all looked to the high stained-glass ceiling atop the centre of the room. Flashes of their early childhoods played out in front of them. The sibling pairs held different versions of each other back then. While Gangisizwe and Nonkululeko remembered fondly how they'd finally found peers on their level, breaking them out of the paranoia and isolation of the lives their parents' careers had created for them, Nthabiseng and Xolani remembered them to be pretentious and aloof snobs who thought the sun shone out of their backsides.

'This is so fucking cool,' Nthabiseng whispered.

'Right?' Gangisizwe whispered back. 'We have to smoke hash in here,' he casually continued in his lowered voice.

Nthabiseng and Xolani's necks snapped back down in unison to look at Gangisizwe. He and Nonkululeko remained with their necks craned towards the ceiling.

'We're definitely doing that,' Nonkululeko whispered. They turned quickly in her direction. She casually dropped her gaze to face them with her forever half-smile and winked.

'You've got it, right?' Gangisizwe asked his little sister.

'I do,' she confirmed.

Nthabiseng and Xolani exchanged alarmed looks and declined to participate. Gangisizwe and Nonkululeko laughed them off, without trying to convince them to change their minds.

'Let's take our places at the couches and do this little catch-up session properly,' Gangisizwe ordered, and they advanced on the four single-seater leather armchairs that surrounded a circular table. A painting on the wall just behind the furniture caught Nthabiseng's eye. She remembered it from her youth but had been too young then to understand the significance of its subjects. She walked over to it and looked back at everyone else with a finger pointed at it.

'Is that …?'

'It is indeed,' Nonkululeko confirmed for Nthabiseng, while she burnt the hash on the tip of a pen before crushing it.

'No fucking way. This is so fucking crazy!' she gasped.

Xolani got off his chair to join her in front of the painting. He was also amazed by its content, having not been able to appreciate it either in his youth. It was an image of men in dishevelled suits in celebration at one end of a table, with others coolly shaking hands at the other end. The exuberant men were white and outnumbered the black men on the other side, who looked to be shaking hands in relief rather than excitement.

'This is the actual fucking negotiating table,' Xolani murmured.

'Pass it here. You've been rolling all afternoon; I'll do this one,' Gangisizwe offered to Nonkululeko.

'After I've just burnt my fingers for this? No fucking way you're taking away my glory,' she replied drily.

Nthabiseng and Xolani exchanged looks of disbelief that a joint was really being prepared in the president's office.

'Was just offering,' Gangisizwe sighed. 'So, Xolani, I heard that song you collaborated with that other white guy on.'

Xolani turned to look at him and was at a loss for a moment, before returning to his seat and putting down his whiskey glass. 'Yeah? What do you think?' he asked warily.

'Hmmm ...' Gangisizwe said, caressing his smooth chin as if there were hair on it. 'Let's smoke this joint first.'

'I'm almost done, geez!' Nonkululeko said through gritted teeth.

'If only the person with the nimblest fingers in the room had been assigned the task,' Gangisizwe sighed into his whiskey glass before taking a sip. Sensing some impending bickering, Nthabiseng took her place on the couch next to Nonkululeko.

'Don't rush it, Nkuli. Every other one you've rolled today has been perfect,' she told her.

'Thank you, and also, here it is!' She proudly held up the sleek, pencil-thin joint. She handed it to Nthabiseng and asked that she do the honours. Nthabiseng looked over at her brother, who seemed to be as resigned as she was. She accepted the gift with one hand, placed her beer down with the other and lit it. They passed it around in silence. When they were finished, they sat in further silence. A comfortable silence that none of them felt the need to intrude on. They surreptitiously caught each other's eyes and shared small, sincere smiles. Nthabiseng and Xolani independently noted to themselves the unaffected manner that their counterparts had taken on since their arrival in the study.

While sitting there and taking in her surroundings, Nonkululeko spoke in a voice barely above a whisper so as not to disturb the library. 'Nthabi, who's that white boy downstairs? The one with a girlfriend.'

Nthabiseng was brought back from her thoughts and considered Nonkululeko for a moment before she answered, 'Oh, Pieter?'

'Yeah, him ...' Nonkululeko said dreamily from her reclined position.

'Shame,' Xolani silently chuckled to himself.

'Oh God, did he say anything embarrassing?' she asked the room.

'Nothing that couldn't be thoroughly addressed,' Gangisizwe smugly declared. Nonkululeko and Xolani giggled at the statement.

'Talk about using a sledgehammer to crack open a nut,' Xolani giggled. Everyone laughed.

'What did I miss and when was this?' she asked.

'You were handling the braai,' Xolani told her.

'It's nothing worth going into really. I'm pretty sure he'll be more responsible with his words around you now,' Gangisizwe laughed.

'Nthabi, how did you inherit him? Cause honestly, he's a mess,' Nonkululeko said, and they all laughed.

'Jeez, why are you guys being so cryptic? Just tell me what he said,' she pleaded, starting to giggle uncontrollably along with everyone else.

'But he's your friend, mos, so you know the potential embarrassment he carries with him,' Gangisizwe added.

'Fuck you guys,' Xolani said through sustained giggling. 'Just leave that fool alone; was the table not enough?' They all laughed harder.

'The problem is not that he's stupid, more that he's just plain clumsy,' Nonkululeko declared to the increasing laughter in the room.

'Yeses!' Gangisizwe sniggered. 'Bull in a china shop, that one.'

The entire room continued to chortle at a controlled volume.

'I was actually watching this comedian the other day and I think his take on ineptitude is perfect for that thing downstairs that you brought us,' Nonkululeko started. The rising laughter had them all holding their stomachs. 'Wait, let me say it. Wait, stop laughing.' They all tried to stop laughing. 'Basically,' she started, but Gangisizwe snorted and they were in another fit of giggles, before they calmed down and let her finish. 'Fuck it, never mind. Gangi ruined it.'

'No!' Nthabiseng pleaded, 'I want to hear this. I already missed whatever happened downstairs.'

They all tried to regain their composure. Nonkululeko straightened her back and took a deep breath. 'Basically, your friend downstairs is the kind of guy who would gift Anne Frank a drumkit.'

Everyone dropped their jaws and gave a collective 'Wow', before they rumbled into a laughter that bounced off the taboo wooden haven they had invaded. It took some time for them to finally recover from their little gossip session.

'Do your guys' parents know that you smoke? I mean y'all smoke so much,' Xolani inquired.

'That's the nice thing about having the favourite sibling be an entire country; it keeps our parents devoted to it and their attention off us. We don't really get to know them, and they don't get to know us. It's a perfect peace for pairs. Mom and Dad; Brother and Sister.'

'Wait, weren't you going to offer us your thoughts on Xolani's music?' Nonkululeko interrupted the conversation.

'Oh yeah,' Gangisizwe remembered. 'It's a really beautiful song, man. Especially for what it means for us.'

'Thanks, man,' Xolani responded shyly.

'The only thing I will say, though,' Gangisizwe continued, 'is that you need to be careful with that kind of shit, man, cause those songs aren't sung without reason, you know what I mean? To sing it for commercial gain might be perceived as opportunistic by some. So you must be ready to answer those kinds of questions when they come, cause a lot of people might take it the wrong way and not understand where you're coming from with it.'

Xolani nodded gravely, 'Yeah, definitely. I appreciate that, man.'

'You've also got to be careful who you make that shit with. I mean to sing from there and have a white boy play the chords for it might cause you a lot of stress. You're giving him a slice of a song that belongs to your people.'

Xolani felt a twinge of irritation that he pushed down, and carried on nodding to indicate he was listening. He drained the remaining whiskey from his glass.

'I'm just trying to look out for you, man. This is shit I feel like you should be thinking about, you know?' Gangisizwe told him. He got up, took Xolani's glass and walked behind the large desk that sat in the corner of the room. He placed his glass on the desk and slid open a globe that held within it a number of liquor bottles. He grabbed a whiskey and replenished Xolani's glass. He put the whiskey back and opened what looked like a cabinet below the globe, but was in fact a fridge and pulled out an ice tray. He dropped a few cubes into the glass, returned the tray to its place and walked back to their space, handing Xolani the glass. Xolani thanked him.

'I'm not sure what you're talking about, to be honest,' Nthabiseng admitted.

'Nthabiseng, are you white?' Gangisizwe asked her.

She looked at him with confusion and annoyance.

'It's not a trick question; it's an honest one and the answer is "No". You're black.'

'Um ...'

'Look, the idea of blackness is a political category and not a fixed identity as purported by the social fiction we're forced to be characters in. Globally, it might be different but in South Africa, if you're not white, then trust that you're black. Blackness is always being renegotiated, depending on the spaces you find yourself in. You can ask your white friends if you want,' Gangisizwe said.

'Ask yourself: if you remained exactly who you were and they didn't know you, but saw you somewhere kind of neutral ... like a park?' Nonkululeko looked to her brother for confirmation, he nodded. 'Imagine they saw you hanging out with a group of people who look like you, it doesn't even have to be friends. Imagine they saw you hanging out with your family in a park, what do you honestly think they'd make of you?'

Nthabiseng and Xolani found themselves getting overwhelmed by the sudden interrogation they were facing. Sensing this, Nonkululeko decided to back off a bit.

'Maybe this isn't the best conversation while we're all this high, Gangi.' She looked at her brother before continuing. 'Sorry guys, I guess we can get kind of intense.'

Gangisizwe also apologised, 'Sorry, I went a little off topic to what I really wanted to say.'

Nthabiseng and Xolani exchanged nervous glances.

Gangisizwe continued, 'So, I'm kind of working for my dad right now ... well, I mean for the party, really, you know what I mean. Anyway, I'm one of the party's arts and culture liaisons. Basically, I secure and strengthen cultural exchanges between us and other countries, and one of the things I've been charged to do is create opportunities for South African artists to access our global networks. Nkuli and I think your band would be perfect as one of our most visible representatives.'

Xolani felt light and wasn't completely sure he understood what he was being told. He looked at Nthabiseng, whose face reflected the disbelief in his own.

'Look, I'm not going to play it safe and these old bastards are so out of touch that they just keep trying to shove wrinkled husks of rainbow nation fame down everyone's throat, which means we young people who need these opportunities end up missing all of them. I obviously don't have that much control just yet, but I was able to wrangle an opportunity to bring on board one act, and I want The Cursed Children of Ham. It's going to take you forever to break out or even be given fair gig fees over here. I think our overseas counterparts will understand South African youth expression better than any of our parents ever could.'

Still gobsmacked, Xolani and Nthabiseng kept looking at each other and then back at Gangisizwe and Nonkululeko, whose smiles were getting wider.

'Wow!' Xolani finally exhaled.

'I'm very fucking confused right now, but at the same time very fucking excited! Gangi, wow!' Nthabiseng shouted and walked over to hug Gangisizwe and then Nonkululeko.

Xolani was still registering it all and stood up feeling faint. Before he could walk over to Gangisizwe, Nthabiseng leapt to hug him and he caught her, almost falling back into the chair. She wrapped her legs around his waist. When she eventually let go, he reached out to hug both Gangisizwe and Nonkululeko.

The quartet smiled at each other awkwardly before Nonkululeko suggested that they return to the party before people started snooping around. Before they left the room, they all agreed not to tell anyone until everything was official. A still-dumbfounded Xolani walked down the stairs with Gangisizwe and Nthabiseng. Nonkululeko walked down the hall to her room.

Downstairs, they arrived to a dance floor in full swing, everyone on the patio dancing wildly and screaming the words, 'Hey ya!' at the top of their lungs. Bell stopped mid-dance and made her way straight to Xolani and kissed him.

'You said you wouldn't be long,' she punched him on the shoulder.

'Sorry, it was my fault. I ended up rambling forever. It's just that it's been so long since I've seen them; we had a lot to catch up on,' Gangisizwe smiled at her. She smiled back at him and told him that he did have a knack of rambling but that he was forgiven.

Gangisizwe joined everyone else dancing, swaying his hips awkwardly and snapping his fingers. He ended up next to Monique who mouthed the words with him.

'I think your friend is a bit of a dick,' Bell told Xolani as she looked up at him with her hands around his neck.

'Yeah, he kind of has that effect on people,' he said as the song finished.

Nonkululeko had made a stealthy re-emergence. Still in her white bikini, she popped open another bottle to attract the desired attention. 'Everybody, please get your flutes. I'm coming around to top everyone up,' she announced in the time it took for the next song to start playing. As she went around filling people's glasses, she also handed them what looked like a ball of crumpled-up Rizla. She told them to swallow it when they all raised their glasses and not to ask questions. She asked everyone to hold the little balls in their palms out in front of them, which they did.

'Bottoms up!' she shouted over the music. Everyone imitated her action of placing the object in her mouth and swallowing it with the Prosecco.

'Why'd I just do that? I just fucking listened; I don't even know what I took,' Bell said to Xolani.

'I do,' Xolani told her with a mischievous smile. 'I know exactly what you took and you're going to love it.' He smiled and kissed her.

*

No one remembered who had suggested going to the pool, but that's where the party ended up. The first person to fall into the pool without encouragement was Nonkululeko. She stood at the pool edge on their arrival, and simply looked like she had allowed her body to succumb to the pull of gravity with the water being her destined landing. The green pool lights kept her well lit beneath the water, where she passively floated for a time without making any effort to kick. Instead, she turned slowly to face everyone who had remained on the edges of the pool. The strands of her braids floated freely around her head and made her appear as if she were a giant, amorphous jellyfish. She remained holding her breath beneath the water, and watched, heard and felt the force of the others she had inspired to jump into the water.

By the time she stood up to draw breath she saw her brother carrying Monique and jumping into the pool with her, fully clothed, waistcoat and all. They all splashed each other with water and found themselves in unexplained and uncoordinated hugs. The warm water and spring heat seemed to be conspiring as they felt waves of energy run over their bodies. They took it in turns to get out of the pool, only to jump back in again.

They found themselves singing about their pursuits for happiness in intervals and laughing with abandon. Pleasant rays of light warmed their limbs and took residence in the stomachs of all who revelled in the pool's merriment. The portable speaker that gave their euphoria a flawless soundtrack carried with it enough power to make them all feel as if they were engulfed by the music; individually connected in their shared experience. Without the words to describe it, they all felt the grand illusion of time swallowing everything and regurgitating fragmented pieces only recognisable to each seeker; yet the pieces had been corroded by a weakened ambition to recall all truth from every manner of perspective. Depending on the clarity and will of the memory's user, the stomach lining of age provided the recollection through the various five sensations, in singular isolations, pairings and at times with the complete submersion into the dimensional reality of the past.

The smell of the pool's chlorine became the indelible beacon of guidance in the memory they were creating while they floated past one another. Without skipping a step, on the beat of the linear chronology of existence, a constant array of infinitesimal multicoloured dots – comprising tiny film strips, in which sat squares of individual memories – danced in front of them, creating the vista through which their eyes perceived their present realities. A constant assault of information preceding that to be taken in and informing that being actioned. It was as if they were all walking through a transparent, metallic celluloid veil, through which their bodies drifted, intermittently conscious of its tangibility.

Xolani couldn't help but feel the joy that had lurked behind his slow comprehension of Gangisizwe's offer in the library. Inside, a smug vindication bolted up and down his spine with the gusto of an Olympic sprinter. He felt redeemed; that he wasn't merely indulging a supposedly meaningless and selfish pipe dream that Uncle Zweli had lambasted. Gangisizwe's offer meant that Uncle Zweli had been wrong to not be proud of him. To have considered him a waste of black skin. He felt assured of his place in the band, not only as the lead singer, but as its founder and leader. Absolved by the knowledge that he'd never have to read another vitriolic review that gnawed at his insecurities for the authenticity of his expression. He had proven that he meant something to the world. He turned to Bell, his sopping dreads flopping over his face.

'I told you you'd love it.'

She kissed him.

Nonkululeko and Nthabiseng had found themselves next to the speaker and cooler box, observing the pool party. Nthabiseng felt her eyes roll back in her skull for half a second before they readjusted themselves. Wet and resting on the grass, the evening's warmth licked away at the droplets on her skin. She smiled in a way that made her believe that she might never stop. She felt she understood her place in the world in that moment. That it was rare to feel so beautiful and be surrounded by the beautiful. Next to her,

Nonkululeko wore a smile that wasn't her constant virtual smirk, but the same smile she had shared with them upstairs. She was preparing another hash joint.

'I have to tell you something that will have to remain between the two of us,' she said conspiringly to Nthabiseng, who returned a lazy smile with half-closed eyes.

'Seriously, this can't ever leave this space. Promise me,' Nonkululeko reaffirmed the importance of the information she wanted share. Nthabiseng promised.

'The whole thing, what we told you guys upstairs … was kind of my idea.'

'What?' Nthabiseng looked at Nonkululeko suspiciously. She was unprepared to give her credit just because she claimed she deserved some.

'Yeah,' she said, as she lit the joint. 'Gangi's been fighting with my parents over the last few months; he wants to drop out of his degree six months shy of getting it. And of course, he's expected to go on and do his honours and master's and so on. But he's just not happy.' She took a drag and passed it to Nthabiseng who lazily turned what felt like her vibrating eyeballs back towards Nonkululeko while she spoke. 'When I heard that song your brother did with that white boy and checked out how much momentum the band had been picking up, I shared it with my mom.' She took the joint that Nthabiseng passed back into her fingers. 'My mom had been confiding in me about how stressful she was finding the tension between my dad and Gangi, so when I shared that with her, she was just too happy to listen.' Nthabiseng was becoming increasingly impressed by Nonkululeko, something she didn't think was possible, because of how impressive she already was.

'Last drag,' Nonkululeko said, as she held her breath after the previous one.

'So, your mom shared the music with your dad and that was it?' Nthabiseng asked before taking her final drag and putting the joint out on the grass.

'Nothing is that simple,' Nonkululeko turned and smiled. 'Uncle Zweli was the key,' she said grinning at Nthabiseng, whose jaw dropped. Uncle Zweli had always been open about his distaste of Xolani's chosen career path and took every opportunity to put him down over it.

'I know,' Nonkululeko nodded excitedly and giggled. Nthabiseng shared her disbelief. 'If it was up to me, I would have tried to pitch it the way you guessed. But my mom offered me wisdom that should help me in my bid for presidency.' They both giggled at the half-joke.

'My dad and Uncle Zweli had been commiserating over their coconut boys who refused to become men. So, she just made them listen to it during one of their discussions. She didn't title it, nor did she tell them who was singing, she just told them to listen. No one said a word, they all just sat there allowing the moment to happen. Uncle Zweli was sobbing, and couldn't believe that Xolani made such beautiful music. She said that he told her that it was the first time he had listened to Xolani's music and regretted not having supported him before. In my father's presence, my mother started toying around with the possibility of internship for the Department of Arts and Culture, and how Gangi would be well suited for such a task. They all came around to the idea somehow and often repeated the song so they could better hear the clarity with which the Xhosa was being sung. Uncle Zweli mused on the idea that maybe Gangisizwe might help Xolani with his own goals. Mom knew that speaking to my dad directly wouldn't have yielded results.'

Nthabiseng was flummoxed by all the information Nonkululeko was dumping on her, as she visualised all the details being described. She realised that she was elated by everything she had heard about how the entire story had unravelled. She looked out at the pool, where everyone danced, screamed and played with a pure joy. She took in all her friends enjoying the company of Nonkululeko's and Gangisizwe's friends. She noted how close Monique and Gangisizwe were as they spoke to each other, their lips almost touching. She watched her brother awkwardly trying to dance in the pool with Bell. She reached for a beer.

Nonkululeko joined her and spoke again, this time

more solemn than conspiring, 'The survivor's guilt that comes with privilege is overwhelming and we all just want to say "Fuck it" and live our lives, free of the suffocating noose of communal burden and expectation.' They both watched their friends frolicking in front of them as she spoke, appreciating the gravity of the situation. 'Jesus, that would be so fucking great!' Nonkululeko sighed before going on. 'But unfortunately, we can't afford to think like that. Especially because of who we are and the expectations that come with that. The world isn't going to suddenly be nice to us, just because we're nice to other people.' They sat in silence for a while, taking in the sounds and sensations of the evening. The grave sermon Nonkululeko had given sat between them, more as a moment of clarity than a burden of responsibility. Nthabiseng finally raised her beer to Nonkululeko who met it with her own.

'But if we keep this to ourselves, what does that make us?' Nthabiseng asked, more philosophically than practically. Nonkululeko's almost smile revisited her face as she looked at Nthabiseng and they both raised their bottles, holding them in mid-air before they met. Nthabiseng noticed Nonkululeko's eyelids flutter and her eyes roll for half a second before she lazily fixed them on her.

'We're children without tongues.'

# Acknowledgements

Thank you to everyone who has had the patience to listen to me harp on about this book for the last forever and a day. To my father and mother, who continue to support me with unwavering intent in everything that I do. My sister, Zukiswa, whose contributions and insights are always on point and without callous disregard, Love is in your face. A huge thank-you to the Pan Macmillan team! Sibongile Machika, who tested the reality of the world I've tried to create. Andrea Nattrass, who is hands down the most thug publisher in the game. Katlego Tapala, my editor, you were about this project from the jump and have ensured that all screws were tightened and panels beaten on what I thought was a wreckage to be written off. I can't thank you enough. Skumbuzo Vabaza, who's always waiting for me to share anything I've written, to the point that he started reading this to baby Amandla. The ever-present Masande and Mbali. Lee and Rofhiwa for staying tuned. Babalwa for sharing your thoughts and honestly supporting this. Michele Perks for being a constant without effort. Khiyara Krige, you made sure that I didn't half-ass this project on initial submission and supported the ideas even when they didn't make sense to me. Thank you so much for the time, patience, love and understanding – you are beyond. I reserve my final bit of gratitude for my kid brother, Lisolomzi Pikoli, better known as Mr Fuzzy Slippers: you're still the closest idea to a superhero that I have.